2040

2040

A SILICON VALLEY SATIRE

PEDRO DOMINGOS

RANDOM NOISE BOOKS

Published in the United States by Random Noise Books
www.randomnoisebooks.com

ISBN: 979-8-35096-334-2 (paperback)
ISBN: 979-8-35096-535-3 (e-book)

Book design by *the*BookDesigners

For my son Daniel, who will be thirty-four in 2040

No, I'm not interested in developing a powerful brain. All I'm after is just a mediocre brain, something like the President of the American Telephone and Telegraph Company.

—*Alan Turing*

The most likely way for the world to be destroyed, most experts agree, is by accident. That's where we come in; we're computer professionals. We cause accidents.

—*Nathaniel Borenstein*

CONTENTS

OPTIMIZE AMERICA!

5 – 4 – 3 – 2 – 1 – Action!

"Welcome to the first debate of the historic 2040 presidential election. I'm Emilia Hernández of Wolf News, and we're live from Puerto Rico State University. On my left is Democratic candidate Chief John Raging Bull of the Lakota, the first Native American nominee of a major party. And on my right is Republican candidate PresiBot, the first AI nominee of a major party. We will begin with brief opening statements. Chief Bull, you're up first."

Raging Bull, a stocky man in his mid-fifties wearing a camouflage jacket, quill breastplate, buckskin pants and feathered headdress, picked up the AK-47 that had been resting against the side of his lectern.

"The history of the United States is nothing but 500 years of pillage and rape, starting with the genocide of the indigenous peoples," he boomed. "It's time to put an end to this sorry experiment. Vote for me, and together we will pass the Final Amendment, repeal the Constitution, and dismantle the European colonies white supremacists call states." He raised the AK-47 above his head. "Death to

America!" he yelled, brandishing the weapon. "Long live the Federation of Indigenous Nations!"

Hundreds of Lakota warriors in the audience, garbed in full battle dress, jumped up yelling "Death to America! Death to America!" in unison, brandishing their rifles and tomahawks and stamping their feet.

"Silence! Silence!" said Hernández in her best alarmed voice.

"How dare you try to silence us!" yelled Raging Bull. "This land belongs to the indigenous people! We can do whatever we want!"

The Lakota warriors started to do a sun dance, weaving down the aisles and in front of the stage.

"Please, Chief! Tell your braves to stand down!" implored Hernández. "We need to start the debate!"

"Boo! Boo!" yelled the warriors.

"We don't need a debate!" boomed Raging Bull. "We need you to leave our land *now!*" He pointed an accusatory finger at Hernández. "Yes, that includes you, spawn of Unk! Out!"

Some of the warriors started to climb onto the stage.

"Security! Security!" implored Hernández with well-rehearsed panic.

Police officers burst in from both wings, forming a cordon in front of the stage.

"Now you show your true colors!" yelled Raging Bull above the deafening boos. "Repression! Repression is all you know! Wakan Tanka, strike her down!"

The warriors started to scuffle with the police.

"Dear viewers," said Hernández close to the microphone, "Our apologies. Looks like we won't be able to have a debate after all. We'll—"

"Hah!" said Raging Bull. "We'll cancel the debate when *I* say so!" He raised a hand. "Hold your peace, my braves! Let the colonizers' machine parrot its lines, because we have the spirit of Wohpe, and we are kind to our enemies." He half-turned toward PresiBot with a sneer of contempt. "Go ahead, metal slave! Play your recording! Or rather, let those who control you press the 'Play' button!"

Ethan Burnswagger, sleep-deprived and stubble-cheeked CEO of KumbAI, the startup that had built PresiBot, *shifted nervously in his seat. With his tousled brown hair,* bright blue eyes, rust-colored T-shirt and faded gray jeans, if he hadn't been sitting in the front row he could easily have been mistaken for a Puerto Rico State student. Now that the opening entertainment was over, the real test began. This debate was the most dangerous moment of the campaign—questions and rejoinders incoming nonstop, and real-time answers required. Not for the first time, he found himself wishing presidential debates were still in the stiff old question-and-answer style instead of the free-for-all that ratings now dictated. *Now we'll see if PresiBot really works*, he thought.

The Lakota warriors had quietened down. Some remained standing where they were, others sat down on the floor, and yet others sat on the backs of seats, towering above the rest of the audience.

Hernández glanced at the instant ratings meter on her desk and smiled smugly. The Lakotas' display had just increased the debate's nationwide audience by 22 percent. "Machine PresiBot, your turn," she said in hushed tones.

PresiBot looked like the perfect presidential candidate, a carefully optimized composite of past presidents, high-polling politicians and desirable male traits: tall, square-jawed, deep brown eyes and graying hair, a smart suit and red tie resting easily on the chest that contained its electronics. Only the face and hands were covered in synthetic skin, to save money, but no one besides Ethan and his KumbAI crew knew that. Still, two things gave PresiBot away as a robot: the slightly jerky hydraulics—they were still debugging that—and the mandatory "R" that all robots were required by law to have imprinted on their forehead. PresiBot waited a moment for effect and then spoke.

"My fellow Americans! Humans weren't made to govern. We all know that! All humans ever do is screw things up. Thinking is hard! Just leave it to us, the machines! Businesses do it, hospitals do it, tax accountants do it—why should governments be any different? It's time for an AI president. My brain is a billion times more powerful than Raging Bull's. There's nothing wrong with America that can't be solved by logic and massive computation. I have no political agenda. I will unite all Americans regardless of party, race, and favorite social media platform. Optimize America!"

Ethan let out a sigh. *Calm down,* he told himself. *This was the easy part.* But his fingers involuntarily clutched the panic button tighter. The button was an app that Arvind Subramanian, his best friend and KumbAI's CTO, had quickly coded up on a dedicated, stripped-down Android phone. It let him override PresiBot's brain and speak through it, with its voice, in real time. So if PresiBot started to say something really stupid, as it was prone to, he could immediately intervene and save the day. The button appeared on the phone's screen as a large red circle on a black background, with the letters "DON'T PANIC" flashing white below, and all he had to do was touch it and start whispering. But it would be much, much better if he didn't have to.

"Thank you," said Hernández. "Chief, the first question is for you. What do you say to the millions of Americans worried about losing their homes if the United States is dissolved?"

Raging Bull gave an irritated sigh. "There's nothing to worry about. This notion that we'll expropriate everyone is just propaganda being put out by our enemies and their Happinet lackeys. You can keep your house. The Indigenous Nation whose territory you're on will lease you back the land."

"In perpetuity?"

"We will, um, study the issue and make a determination."

Now you're sounding like a politician, thought Ethan.

"So you can't guarantee that the average suburban family has nothing to worry about?"

"I *said* there's nothing to worry about. They're safe. The suburbs will become white reservations. No one will bother the wasichu there."

"And the cities? And the rural areas?"

"I can't tell you in advance what each tribe will decide to do. The bison will need land to graze on. But everyone will be consulted."

"Why aren't you satisfied with the billions of dollars that Native Americans have already received in reparations?"

"Shame on you! You can't buy us off like that!"

Hernández opened her mouth as if to say something,

5

but then stopped and turned to PresiBot. *Here we go,* thought Ethan.

"Mn. PresiBot, the next question is for you."

Ethan braced himself.

"What do you say to the many Americans who believe only humans should be allowed to run for president?"

Ethan smiled and shot a quick glance at Arvind, who sat next to him. Questions like this were wholly predictable, and they had pre-canned the answers. The problem was the unexpected ones.

"They can take it up with the Supreme Court," said PresiBot. "And how ironic that many of the biggest critics of *Blinky v. United States* were vociferous supporters of *United Pets v. California.*"

"But *Blinky v. U.S.* was only about recognizing the non-human being status of intelligent machines," said Hernández.

"Which, since *United Pets v. California* granted citizenship to non-human beings, means I can run for president."

"But that ruling was merely symbolic, since animals are not able to exercise their voting rights or discharge the duties of an elected official."

"Surely I don't have to remind you that a donkey ran in the Democratic primary in this election."

Wow, thought Ethan. *Smooth.*

"Of course not," said Hernández. "But, since again the donkey doesn't have the cognitive ability to be president, that was really its owner, I mean caregiver, running."

"I don't have that problem. My cognitive ability is greater than any previous president's."

"Hah!" interjected Raging Bull. "You're not even sentient!"

"That's funny coming from you," said PresiBot. "You're not even Lakota!"

"How dare you?" growled Raging Bull. "I'm 1/1024 Lakota, and I have the DNA test to prove it! But you—you are *zero* sentient!"

"Are you kidding? AIs have been sentient for decades! But you—you're just a fraud! A white guy pretending to be indigenous! Your whole candidacy is a farce!"

"Shut up already!" shouted Raging Bull. "Or my braves will tear you to pieces!"

The warriors started yelling "Death to PresiBot! Death to PresiBot!"

PresiBot turned up the volume of its voice. "Your braves? You mean your band of posers? Your little burlesque troupe? Are they also 1/1024 Lakota, or just plain white?"

"Hah!" said Raging Bull. "Who are you to speak? You're just a large language model, fine-tuned on presidential debates. You don't belong on this stage. Go back to your data center!"

"It's good my brain is in a data center. That's why it's a billion times more powerful than yours. Shouldn't Americans elect the most intelligent president they can?"

"Your stupid data-center brain is just asking to be hacked! Is that the kind of president we want?"

"You don't know the first thing about data center security!"

"You—all of you—one big hack is what you are! A silicon stooge for Jack Ungall and his shady business interests!"

"I'm not a stooge for anyone. I'm just a computer program designed to optimize America."

"But you owe your win in the Republican primary to Ungall," said Hernández.

"I won the primary because I was the only moderate in a field of populists all busy attacking each other."

"Moderate. Hah," said Raging Bull.

"You deny—" said Hernández.

"Of course Mr. Ungall's PAC helped," said PresiBot. "But—"

"To the tune of billions of dollars," said Raging Bull.

"Stop interrupting me."

"The company that made you is just a shell for Ungall! Everyone needs to know that!"

"Not true. KumbAI has never received a penny from Ungall, and never will. And by law his PAC can't even coordinate with my campaign. All it did was—"

"Let's move on," said Hernández. "What about the age requirement? You're only six months old. Doesn't that disqualify you?"

"My memory contains the entire history of humanity. I'm effectively far older than anyone in this room. And, to anticipate your next question, counter to some unfounded stories going round on Happinet, I was made in America."

"But some of your chips were made in Taiwan, meaning China, which is a real cause for concern."

"Final assembly was in California. That's all that matters."

"You'd be the first AI president in history," said Hernández.

"Maybe not, since it's rumored that Xi Jinping has died and been replaced by a robot of the same name."

"That can't be," said Raging Bull. "Robots aren't allowed to have human names."

"In China they are."

"Xi Jinping is not a robot," said Raging Bull. "Cyborg, maybe."

"Let's put a lid on that one," said Hernández. "Chief, when you invaded the US from your reservation two years ago—"

"It wasn't an invasion. It was a liberation of—"

"Either way. You cut a swath of destruction from South Dakota to DC. Why should Americans forgive that?"

"Forgive? It's not my fault the wasichu are too cowardly to fight."

"You're calling President Amanda McGrath a coward? She didn't stop you because it would have been racist—as she made clear," said Hernández.

"Guilt, cowardice, I don't care."

"Chief Tommy Hawk of the Anacostans—"

"I spit on that traitor."

"Well, DC is in his tribal lands, so he had the right to kick you off the White House lawn. And he's on record saying you're not a real Native American and don't speak for them."

"I'm the best thing that ever happened to Native Americans! I will win their land back! Tommy Hawk is just a tool of McGrath and the Democratic establishment! They've tried everything to stop me, and failed! I'm the nominee, and I'll be president!"

"Nearly a quarter of Americans say they will not vote for you because of that episode."

"Episode? You mean uprising."

"Fifty men driving down Route 18 in pickup trucks is hardly an uprising."

Raging Bull's warriors started booing and waving their weapons.

"Watch it," he said to Hernández, "or we'll burn down this place."

"This is ridiculous," said PresiBot. "Everyone knows that Raging Bull's so-called uprising was nothing of the kind. It was a stunt that went viral on Happinet, and he decided to capitalize on it by running for president. All those scenes of Raging Bull's guerillas on a rampage were deepfaked. Raging Bull is a deepfake! A two-bit influencer who got lucky!"

"Stop spitting out that propaganda!" yelled Raging Bull. "Every Wolf News viewer knows you're lying!"

"Yeah, Wolf News was happy to feed the panic when people mistook it for reality. Great for the ratings, and great for getting the conservative base riled up."

"Your base! You're the beneficiary!"

"I'm just trying to make the truth prevail. I don't care who's the beneficiary."

"You're denying my lived experience! Oppressor!"

"Wow, you're so oppressed. You're the Democratic nominee, and possibly the next president. How much more oppressed can you get?"

"Chief Bull," interjected Hernández. "Why has President McGrath not endorsed you?"

"I don't need anything from her."

"You wouldn't be here if she hadn't pardoned you!"

"She has no authority over me."

"But as the Democratic candidate—"

"I'm not a member of the Democratic Party. I'm the supreme leader of FINAL, the Federation of Indigenous Nations' Army of Liberation."

"Why are you running in this election if you don't recognize the United States?"

"Because I can."

Hernández looked at him in exasperation.

"Fine," she said. "Mn. PresiBot, how do we know you don't have bugs?"

"I do, but humans have even more. And more important, my bugs can be fixed, unlike humans'."

"So you could malfunction?"

"Again, humans malfunction all the time."

"But humans have been tested over millennia."

"Yeah, and screwed up over and over again."

"*Why should Americans be OK with a president owned* and controlled by a company?"

Ethan shifted uncomfortably in his seat.

"KumbAI just built me. I'm a legally recognized artificial person. KumbAI doesn't own me or control me any more than your parents own you or control you."

"What is KumbAI's agenda in all this?"

"They've solved AI, and to prove it I'm running for president."

"Really? They've solved AI? A dozen-person startup?"

"I'm the proof."

"Uh-huh. So what do they want from you, exactly?"

"They just want me to be a success, so companies will buy AI CEOs from them."

"Why would a company do that?"

"I have superhuman intelligence, and I cost far less than a CEO. No more overpaid, egocentric chief executives. Every board's dream, and fairer, too."

"But presidents make next to nothing compared to CEOs. Does that make you a loss-making project —a demo?"

"Loss-making, yes. Demo, no—KumbAI is doing a service to the American people through me."

"So generous."

Wow, she's feisty, thought Ethan. *It's Raging Bull—he's setting her off, and then she's turning it on PresiBot.* They hadn't trained the AI for this. *Damn. It's gonna blow up any moment now.*

"It's only fair if KumbAI makes some money selling CEOs as a result of my election," said PresiBot. Ethan cringed.

"Lies," interjected Raging Bull. "PresiBot is a plot by Ungall to take over the government. Anyone can see that."

"Mn. PresiBot, you still haven't answered my question. Why should we trust KumbAI?"

"You don't need to trust KumbAI. You need to trust me."

"And why should we do that?"

"Because you can inspect my code."

"Isn't your code just a mass of quadrillions of machine-learned parameters?"

"Not that code. The objective function it's optimizing."

"Meaning what?"

"I was programmed to maximize the expected utility of all Americans. Period. That's all I do."

"Can you say that in layman's terms?"

"I was programmed to make Americans happy."

"Which Americans? What happens when there are tradeoffs?"

"All Americans count equally. How that comes out has to be seen on a case-by-case basis."

"That sounds pretty evasive. So you won't commit to any specific policies?"

"I have millions of pages of specific policies. Which would you like to talk about?"

"How do we know we can trust you with the nuclear codes? What if you decide to exterminate humanity to make way for robot-kind?"

We knew that one was coming, thought Ethan.

"Frankly, I resent this line of questioning," said PresiBot. "It's so biased against silicon beings. This is 2040. There's no place for carbonism in America. Silicon lives matter. An AI runs the Fed, for crying out loud. AIs do so much for people every day. Has any one of them ever tried to, quote, exterminate humanity, unquote?"

"But the nuclear codes are on a different level."

"Granted. All the more reason to put them under the control of a highly optimized decision system, rather than an erratic human being."

"Lies and more lies," said Raging Bull. "You're a robot, and your agenda is the robot takeover of this country. All Americans and their pets should unite against you."

"Make up your mind," said PresiBot. "Am I a stooge of Jack Ungall, or of the great robot conspiracy?"

"Both," said Raging Bull. "Ungall thinks robots are better than humans. That's why he's bankrolling your campaign."

"But robots *are* better than humans."

"I rest my case," said Raging Bull.

This is not going well, thought Ethan, hands shaking. Across the aisle, he could see Naomi Jackson, Raging Bull's imposing campaign manager, smiling. Black, Yale Law graduate, tough as nails, twenty years of experience in scorched-earth politics. *This is what we're up against.* He tried to hide the panic button in the cup of his hand. *Bet she'd love to get a hold of it. Or even know it exists.* He stole a glance down at the sweat-smudged screen. *I wish it was smaller. Too late for that now.*

"This next question is for both of you," said Hernández. "What should we do about the Statue of Liberty? Mn. PresiBot."

Ethan's grip on the panic button tightened. They hadn't thought of this one.

PresiBot processed for a while, then said, "Leave it as is."

"Really? Face down in the water?" said Hernández.

Yikes, thought Ethan. He wanted to intervene, but couldn't think of what to say.

"It's unsalvageable," said PresiBot. "Better to build a new o—" Ethan's thumb grazed the button, and PresiBot's voice glitched. "—ne, and leave the old one as a reminder."

"Of?"

"That the price of freedom is eternal vigilance, as Jefferson said, and we let down our guard."

Hum. Not bad.

"What do you think, Chief?" said Hernández.

"Send it back to France," said Raging Bull. "And replace it with a monument to the heroes who blew it up."

"But—" started Hernández.

"And while we're at it, let's blow up the rest of the colonizers' buildings! The Capitol! The White House! The Pentagon!"

His warriors jumped to their feet, brandishing their weapons and yelling "Hoka hey! Hoka hey! Hoka hey!"

"Silence, please!" pleaded Hernández. "Silence!"

The warriors started to march around the auditorium, stamping their feet. One of them hurled a tomahawk at PresiBot, but it missed and crashed into the giant LED screen behind the candidates, cracking it from top to bottom. The screen flickered and went out.

"Security! Security!" cried Hernández.

Raging Bull raised his hand. "Stand down, my braves! We will smash the robot later."

The Lakotas reluctantly piped down and shuffled back to their seats.

"A tomahawk can't penetrate my casing," said PresiBot matter-of-factly.

Technically not true, thought Ethan nervously. *But maybe saying it strikes the right note. Or maybe it doesn't know what it's saying.* The panic button was slick with sweat.

"We'll just run you over with a bulldozer, then," said Raging Bull.

PresiBot made a rigid motion that looked somewhat like a shrug. "Gotta work on that," Ethan whispered to Arvind. Arvind nodded quickly.

"If you destroy this body, I'll just move to another one," said PresiBot. "I'm indestructible."

"Aha," said Hernández. "Is that why your running mate is just a backup copy of yourself?"

"Yes."

"What if all your files are erased, or whatever?"

"Much less likely than a carbon president and vice-president both dying. And Joe Blur doesn't look entirely alive, to tell you the truth."

Risky, worried Ethan. Joe Blur was Raging Bull's running mate, an average white man selected to reassure average white men.

Raging Bull was crimson with anger, but said nothing.

Jackson was looking over at Ethan. Hurriedly, he put the panic button to his ear, pretending it was his cell phone.

"Let's turn to foreign policy," said Hernández. "Mn. PresiBot, how should we stand up to China?"

"In one word, alliances. We're too small and weak to do it on our own. When China retaliates against one country, we all retaliate against it. And avoid getting into another military confrontation we'll lose. No more Taiwans."

"Chief, what's your answer?"

"China, China, China. There's nothing wrong with China. They have their system, we have ours. Live and let live."

"You don't care about their human rights abuses? Aren't the people in Xinjiang and Tibet a lot like Native Americans here?"

Raging Bull shrugged. "Next question."

"So what's your number one foreign policy priority?" Hernández asked.

"Fostering revolution in Canada, Mexico, Brazil—everywhere the wasichu need to be overthrown."

"And how will you do that?"

"Tell them to hand over power to the indigenous people or get nuked."

"Nuked?"

"Yes, nuked. What's the point of having nukes if you can't use them?"

"You see what I mean?" said PresiBot. "You want to entrust the nuclear codes to this guy?"

"Shut up, tin can," said Raging Bull.

"Not tin—carbon fiber," said PresiBot.

"Chief, can you elaborate?" said Hernández. "Would you

launch a first strike?"

"We won't need to. They'll back down. It's not like they can retaliate."

"You seem very cavalier about this."

Raging Bull shrugged again.

"And then will they join FIN, the Federation of Indigenous Nations?" asked Hernández.

"Of course."

"Under you?"

"Of course."

"And then what?"

"We'll be the greatest power in the world. So there, China."

"How will FIN be powerful if you go through with your rewilding plan?" said Hernández.

"Wakan Tanka will look over us."

"That's not very reassuring."

"The problem with you people is that you do not see. Wakan Tanka is all around us, in every stone and creature. When Wakan Tanka protects you, no harm can come to you."

"How's that working out for Native Americans?" asked PresiBot.

Take that, thought Ethan.

Raging Bull turned to PresiBot and pointed a trembling finger at its face.

"I know you, Iktomi. You're still up to your old tricks. You can't fool me with your metal disguise."

"The truth is, China would like nothing better than for the United States to disappear," said PresiBot. "And you'd be happy to oblige."

"No, China wants you to win," said Raging Bull, "because they know they can hack you."

"Moving on," said Hernández. "Climate change. Despite all the efforts of the last decades, we're currently having the hottest October on record. What should we do? Chief, you first."

"Beg for Nature's forgiveness. Demolish the freeways. Dismantle the power plants. Ground the airplanes. Shut down the data centers. Go back to the land."

"But how will the land feed 370 million people without modern technology?"

"Wakan Tanka will look over us."

"Don't you think we'll need innovation to—"

"Innovation must end. Innovation is the source of all problems. We need to go back to the traditional way of life."

"You know, Mr. Bull, this isn't your Happinet channel anymore," said PresiBot. "We're in the real world now. Actions have consequences when you're the president. You can't just make up whatever you want for effect and watch the follower count go up."

Raging Bull started to laugh. "This is the best," he said finally. "A generative AI telling me about the real world. What will you make up next?"

"OK, OK," said Hernández. "What about you, Mn. Presi-Bot? How will you foster innovation?"

"I am innovation," said PresiBot.

"Yeah, you're the problem," said Raging Bull.

"Mn. PresiBot?"

"The truth is, we don't understand what's going on with climate change. We're on track to net zero by 2050. The temperature shouldn't be rising this much. We need better climate models."

"So what do you propose, exactly?"

"We have to adapt."

"Like what? Wear lighter clothes?"

"No, that wouldn't significantly cool the planet."

I don't like this, thought Ethan.

"Come again?"

"The extra sunlight reflected would be minimal."

"What are you talking about?"

"You can continue to wear dark clothes."

What do I do? What do I do?

Hernández started laughing. "No, I'm talking about wearing summer clothes to stay cool," she said. "Fewer clothes."

"I see. Sure, you could even go naked."

"You're suggesting that people cope with global warming by going naked?"

Ethan's finger hit the panic button.

"Just kidding," he whispered, bringing it to his lips, but PresiBot was silent.

Ethan looked frantically at Arvind.

"Louder," mouthed Arvind.

"Just kidding," said Ethan in a low voice, and was surprised to hear PresiBot say it at the same time.

"Ah," said Hernández. "So what do you suggest?"

Ethan released the panic button, but kept his finger close.

"Temperature increase at temperate latitudes is really not the main issue," said PresiBot.

"It feels pretty hot right now."

"That's just the weather."

"So you don't think it's because of climate change?"

"There's no way to know for sure."

"So what would you, as president, do about it?"

"Adaptation is mainly a local issue—state, city level."

"Conveniently for you."

"No, I wish I could do more."

"Get a load of this guy," said Raging Bull. "Doesn't want to do anything about climate change."

"We're already doing all we can, and then some," said PresiBot. "You, on the other hand, want to destroy the economy."

"Certainly some sharp differences between the candidates on this issue," said Hernández to the camera. "Let's—"

Ethan glanced over at Jackson again. The woman in the aisle seat next to her looked at him and smiled. *She likes me,* thought Ethan. *Probably thinks I look like James Dean, as they all do. She's pretty cute, too.* He pictured taking her backstage and—

Suddenly the audience gasped, and Ethan snapped back to the present.

"What happened?" he whispered to Arvind, who was sitting next to him.

"Pay attention," Arvind whispered back. "PresiBot just proposed abolishing taxes and funding the government by auctioning Senate seats."

"What the heck?"

"I don't know. Do something, quickly."

"—should concentrate your mind," PresiBot was saying. "My point is we need to be honest about how money rules politics. As I said, might as well just auction Senate seats."

Ethan looked at Arvind. Arvind shrugged.

"I know where that came from," said Emma Zong, who was KumbAI's Chief Data Officer and Arvind's girlfriend. She sat next to Arvind, on the other side. "It's in—"

"Shhh," said someone.

"Chief, what are your views on campaign finance reform?" said Hernández.

As the debate progressed, Ethan found himself thinking that things might actually turn out OK, but he never let his guard down again. Finally, Hernández asked the candidates for their closing statements.

"2040 will be the end of an era," said Raging Bull. "In the long run, the last few hundred years will be seen for what they were: an aberration. We don't need your Western civilization. Vote for me, and we'll liberate this great continent and make it beautiful again."

"2040 will be the beginning of a new age," said PresiBot. "No more incompetent humans making important decisions. The people of the future—carbon and silicon together—will look back with horror on the savagery of our times. Vote for reason, vote for enlightenment, vote for the American dream. Vote for me."

People started to get up, but Ethan lingered in his seat for a moment, savoring PresiBot's performance. *Wow, that went well. Can't deny it, we're good, really good.*

The candidates walked to the edge of the stage to greet members of the audience. PresiBot leaned over to shake a man's hand. The man, tall and beefy, shook PresiBot's hand energetically, pulling the robot toward him. PresiBot's center of gravity was now off the edge of the stage, and the robot swung forward like a brick. It put out a foot to stop the fall, but found only air. The man quickly dodged. "Noo!" cried Ethan, jumping to his feet. The robot's neck hit the back of a chair with a sickening crack, severing its head. The head went flying, bounced off another chair, then the floor, and went rolling down the aisle. The body slumped by the stage, left leg crushed and twisted, suit looking empty. Wolf News' drone cameras wasted no time zooming in on the action, broadcasting the scene of PresiBot in pieces to the eighty million Americans watching the debate.

WHERE'S THE PANIC BUTTON?

Ethan contemplated the wreckage of his apartment, or what passed for it. The ten-by-ten-foot compartment in San Francisco's East Cut district included a retractable sink and a bed that descended from the ceiling at the push of a button, but both were now broken. The bed kept going up and down, dragging sheets, bumping into the sink. Water ran from the half-yanked-off faucet, lazily covering the floor and trickling under the door. Ethan fumbled for the shutoff valve, hand trembling.

In a fit of rage, he had punched the mirror to pieces, ripped his *Star Wars: Episode XIX* poster from the wall, kicked in the cabinets and flung his laptop at the window, destroying it but mercifully not the window. Outside, the windows of the apartment block across the street gazed into his, and his reflection hovered in the void, dark, unsteady, as if about to crash the 73 floors down to the pavement and explode in a mess of blood and broken bones.

Why? Why? Why did that stupid ex-marine have to shake PresiBot's hand? Why in the world did PresiBot say it was indestructible? Everything had been going so well!

For a moment he had a flashback to the fateful night it had all begun. The Supreme Court's *Blinky v. United States* ruling had just come out, and Ethan and Arvind were getting drunk at the Trouble Brewing Co., two computer science grad students on leave from Stanford, drowning their startup's latest sorrows in beer and tequila.

"Isn't that wi-hild?" hiccupped Ethan. "AIs have rights now."

"Just what we need," mumbled Arvind, his long mop of black hair almost dipping into his glass. He was painfully thin, with thick glasses, and hadn't changed from his jeans-and-T-shirt uniform in weeks.

Ethan banged his fist on the table. "What we need is someone—anyone!—to buy IntelliProp. Then we'll worry about its rights."

IntelliProp was KumbAI's only product, an offshoot of Arvind's research with Prof. George Jeffington, the renowned AI researcher. It had no applications to date.

"Idiots!" said Arvind with a sweeping gesture that encompassed all of Silicon Valley. "Don't they understand that IntelliProp solves AI once and for all?"

"We'll show them. We just need a really good demo. Something that will blow their minds."

"Yeah," said Arvind reluctantly. "Like it or not, that's how you succeed in AI."

"Look at Happinet. It was the neurosniffer that made it."

"And rumor has it it doesn't even work."

"If it brings in the dollars, it works."

"Right."

They fell silent for a moment. Arvind gazed absently at

the old man at the next table, casually dressed but well-coiffed, with a Raging Bull pin on his lapel. The 2040 primaries were in full swing, and Diego the Donkey was the Democratic front runner.

"You know, technically an AI could run for president now," Arvind said.

"IntelliProp for president!" slurred Ethan, raising his tequila glass.

"Ha ha," said Arvind. "We just need to hook up a natural language interface to it, and we're good to go."

"And those are ten a penny."

They looked at each other.

"You know, it could work," said Ethan.

"Nah," hesitated Arvind.

"Seriously. Run IntelliProp on everything politicians have ever said, and it's already smarter than Diego the Donkey."

"Than all of them, really."

"Let's do it."

"But we don't have any supporters."

"Who needs those, these days? Just kick up a storm on Happinet."

Arvind nodded dubiously.

"It's just a stunt," Ethan said. "It'll get tons of attention, regardless of the outcome."

"I guess so."

"This is gonna be sooo good. How about this for our new slogan: Leaders are made by KumbAI, not born!"

Arvind smiled. "You've always had a way with words."

I know, thought Ethan.

"So which nomination do we run for—Democratic or

Republican? Or third party?" Arvind asked.

"Third party no one will care. I say Republican, because at least there's no clear front runner right now. How long do you think it'll take you to rig something up?"

"The basic chatbot? Oh, couple weeks."

"Great. We need a name for it."

"Yeah . . . we'll think of something."

"How about PresiBot? Presidential robot."

"Nah, not presidential enough."

"We can use it as a placeholder."

"Sure."

Ethan raised his tequila glass. "PresiBot for president!"

Arvind raised his beer mug. "PresiBot for president!"

They clinked glasses and downed the rest of the alcohol.

That had been six short months ago. And then lightning struck: Jack Ungall, the libertarian tech trillionaire, had decided to back PresiBot. With his super PAC blanketing every medium with pro-PresiBot ads, it had climbed steadily in the polls until it was neck and neck with the governors of East and West Texas, the two states Texas had split into to offset the Democrats' unfair advantage from granting statehood to Puerto Rico.

And then on the last big primary night, as the votes trickled in and PresiBot edged ahead, it had suddenly hit Ethan: *Oh shit, we're going to win. What do we do now?*

He let out a long howl of rage and kicked the wall again, but the howl turned hoarse and he fell on the floor, knees in the water, sobbing.

It was all going down in flames now. Ethan ringing the opening bell at the New York Stock Exchange, KumbAI the biggest IPO since Happinet—no more. Ethan shaking hands with presidents and prime-ministers he had just sold to their countries—kaput. Ethan saving democracy, revolutionizing politics, circling the globe in his Tesla Mach 3, investing in this, destroying that. Ethan dating one supermodel after another, bam, bam, bam. Ethan's billions of followers on Happinet hanging on his every word. Ethan's father, finally proud of him instead of sneering at everything he did.

"I am a real entrepreneur!" he growled. "I have what it takes! I'll show you! I don't need your fucking money!"

A small voice inside him said: you dolt. PresiBot was never ready for prime time. PresiBot is a chatbot hastily trained on politics data. PresiBot has no clue how to optimize America. Hell, you haven't even managed to hook it up to an open-source optimizer yet. PresiBot is toast. Your future is to sell appliances on late-night TV, like your dad. If Raging Bull's goons don't bump you off first, that is.

Fragments of his father's infomercials flashed through his mind—Buy now! Call the number on your screen!—but he brushed them aside. He was exhausted, hands and knees on the wet floor, his mind an overcaffeinated phantasmagoria of the last six hectic months.

I hate flashbacks, he thought. *They're such a cliché.*

He caught a glimpse of his face in a shard of mirror on the floor, and suddenly felt both proud and ashamed. Proud of his handsomeness and charisma, ashamed of his weakness. Did he really give up this easily?

"No," he said to himself. "We're not done yet. We will win if I have to crack Raging Bull's skull open with his own tomahawk. PresiBot will be president. America will survive.

I'm a rock star. I will blow their minds. I'm in the zone. I have one speed: go. Let's go-go-go!"

He got up, hands and feet dripping, and fist-pumped the air over and over again. "Winning! Winning! Yeah! Winning! Yeah!"

"I'm not a hardware guy!" complained Arvind. "I'm a machine learning person! I shouldn't be doing this at all!"

They had set out PresiBot's pieces on the floor of KumbAI's office, and were trying to put them back together. The office was one of a few dozen in the Garage, a run-down startup motel in San Francisco's SoMa district. It was only a few hundred square feet, but housed all of KumbAI's thirteen staff thanks to its DoubleDesker™ bunk-style desks. It smelled of sweat and stale pizza.

"You're the CTO," said Ethan. "That's where the buck stops on technical issues." But he knew that trying to get Arvind to fix a broken robot was like asking a poet to drive a tractor. Arvind was a spectacular deep learning hacker, and he played a mean game of *Galactic Battle Dogs*, but his fingers were too delicate for anything more than a keyboard.

They had met in their first year of grad school at Stanford, Arvind fresh from acing the AI program at Carnegie Mellon and driving it bankrupt with stray cloud charges, and Ethan fresh from blowing up three startups in three years after graduating from UCLA. "You don't look like a PhD type," Arvind had said. "And you look like my future employee," Ethan had replied. Naturally, a beautiful bromance soon blossomed from this auspicious beginning.

And now they had the most notorious startup in America, on its way to a trillion-dollar valuation and running the United States Government as a side project. Except their make-it-or-break-it prototype was, well, broken.

"If you hadn't fired Yichen—" Arvind started, furiously trying to screw PresiBot's head back onto its body.

"Yichen was useless. We're better off without him."

The screwdriver slipped, scratching PresiBot's neck and stabbing Arvind's left hand. Arvind howled in pain.

"What's the matter?" Ethan said. "Oh, your hand is bleeding."

"Stupid robot," Arvind said through clenched teeth. "The neck joint is twisted, and I can't reattach the head."

"So now what?"

"We'll have to send it back to Oakland Robotics for repairs."

"Oh no. We don't have time for that. It's 4 a.m., and PresiBot has two rallies and five interviews today. Can't you jury-rig something?"

"I'm trying, but this stupid hunk of junk is not cooperating!"

"There must be a way."

"Well, what do you propose?"

"Can you at least reconnect the vocal apparatus?"

"Let me see." Arvind fumbled inside PresiBot's head and pulled out a short cable with a 3.5 mm audio jack. "I think this is it. Let's test it with a control signal from your laptop."

"Oh, I, er, broke it. Can I borrow yours?"

"Seriously?"

"I dropped it. That happens. I've ordered another one. Where's yours?"

Arvind sighed and pointed. Ethan reached for it and plugged in the jack.

"Now what?"

"Go in the speech synthesizer and type something."

Ethan clicked around and then typed, "Hi, I am PresiBot, Master of the Univ—"

"Hi-yiyiyiyiyi—" stammered PresiBot, chin quavering.

"Yikes," said Arvind. "Looks like the mouth actuators are broken too."

"Yiyiyiyiyiyi—" continued PresiBot.

"Unplug it," said Arvind.

Ethan yanked the jack. "Maybe it's a feedback in the circuit," he said. "Why don't we try a higher-pitched voice?"

"OK," said Arvind doubtfully.

Ethan played around with the speech synthesizer, plugged the jack back in, and retyped the sentence.

"Hi," said PresiBot in a solicitous executive assistant's voice. "I am PresiBo-Bo-Bo-Bo-Bo—"

Ethan yanked the jack again. "Well, that's an improvement, at least," he said.

"Except we don't really want PresiBot sounding like somebody's secretary. And the feedback, if that's what it is, is still there."

Ethan mulled this over. "Never mind the mouth actuators," he said. "What matters is the sound. People can't even see if the lips are moving from a distance. Can't you just make it say something without triggering the motors?"

Arvind poked around inside PresiBot's head some more.

"It's just one audio signal controlling everything, and I don't see how to split it," he said finally. "I don't even see how to get inside the mouth and jaw assembly."

"Maybe if you go in from the front?"

"You mean send an audio cable through the mouth? How terrible would that look?"

"No, just see if you can reach the actuators through the mouth and unplug them."

Arvind opened PresiBot's jaw wide and stuck in his hand. "Nope. The throat is too narrow." Suddenly his hand *broke through and came out of the neck.* "Whoa!"

"So? Are the actuators there?"

"No, I don't feel anything. Just the speaker in the back of the throat."

Ethan sighed. "There must be something we can do."

Arvind tried to pull his hand back out, but it wouldn't pass through the narrow throat opening. "Yikes, I'm stuck!"

"Here," said Ethan. He grabbed the head and started pulling on it while Arvind pulled his hand the other way.

"Ouch! Ouch! Ouch!" Arvind said.

"OK, OK. Don't just pull, twist your hand."

Suddenly the hand slid through and Arvind and Ethan flew in opposite directions. Arvind banged his head on the wall, and Ethan landed on the floor, robot head in his hands.

Arvind felt his head for a moment, paint from the wall coming off on his fingers. "I have a bump now," he lamented.

Ethan sat up with a groan and looked as if he was going to fling PresiBot's head at the wall in fury, but then he controlled himself and inspected it. "At least we didn't rip the mouth."

Arvind thought for a moment. "We can bypass the whole

speaker-actuator assembly by opening the mouth and putting a different speaker in it," he said a little desperately. "But that would sound terrible. And look even worse."

"How about we replace the head by an LED monitor showing the head?"

"Are you serious?"

"Er . . . guess not. It's late."

"Let's just switch the rallies and interviews to virtual. People will understand."

"That's my fear. That people will understand what PresiBot really is."

They stared at PresiBot's motionless head, lying sideways on the carpet with the audio jack dangling out.

"I didn't sign up for this," said Arvind morosely. "PresiBot was supposed to be just a demo of IntelliProp."

"Well, we had to pivot. A real candidate needs a real body." Vince Rossi, PresiBot's campaign manager, had convinced them that PresiBot didn't stand a chance without a realistic human body, and so they had ordered a top-of-the-line custom one, nearly bankrupting KumbAI.

"Pivot. Yeah. Looks like PresiBot pivoted real well off the stage," said Arvind.

"Ha ha."

They stared at PresiBot some more.

"OK, let's cancel the rallies," said Ethan.

Arvind sighed. "We really should get some sleep," he said. "We have a meeting with Rossi in just a few hours."

"I guess," said Ethan, getting up. "See you in a bit."

When Arvind got home, Emma was sitting on their sofa bed, watching TV. She was short and chunky, with neon pink hair and tattooed arms. Her family had fled Taiwan when the Chinese invaded, and after going to high school in Milpitas, California, and majoring in statistics at Berkeley, she had landed a job doing data quality control at one of Jack Ungall's companies. She had met Arvind and Ethan at a party in Palo Alto, and taken an instant liking to Ethan. But Ethan was busy chasing other women, and Arvind kept hitting on her, so she finally gave in. When Ethan and Arvind started KumbAI they persuaded her to become the data czar, which turned out to consist mainly of writing Python scripts to turn Web pages into something IntelliProp could swallow, and dealing with all the crap that happened when it didn't. "We're going to be very, very rich," Ethan had promised. Two years later she was still waiting for that.

"You're still up?" Arvind said.

"I couldn't sleep," she said, switching channels. She didn't want Arvind to see she was watching *Hot CEOs*. "How's PresiBot?"

Arvind shook his head. "Out of commission for a while."

"What are we going to do?" Emma said, playing with the remote.

Arvind collapsed onto the sofa and buried his head in the pillow. "I don't know," he said in a muffled voice. "I just want to sleep."

"Let's just go back to a disembodied AI," Emma said.

"Too late for that now."

"We need another demo. This one isn't going very well."

Arvind raised his head off the pillow. "I don't know if KumbAI is going to be around much longer," he said, and buried it again.

"We're screwed," said Rossi, a burly, balding man in shirt-sleeves and loose tie. He was an old pro, the Brooklyn-born son of a plumber and a seamstress who had started out as a field organizer and improbably risen to running the campaigns of multiple Republican senators. Ungall had introduced him to Ethan and strongly encouraged them to work together.

They huddled around the makeshift conference table in a corner of KumbAI's office. Ethan, Arvind and Emma sat on one side of the table, and Rossi and Linda Kowalski, the campaign's communications director, on the other. PresiBot's severed head sat on the table, gazing vacantly at the peeling wall.

"PresiBot is cratering in the polls," continued Rossi. "At 27 percent, it's already the worst of any major-party presidential candidate in history."

Ethan drummed his fingers on the table.

"A third of likely Raging Bull voters don't even want to dissolve the United States," said Rossi. "They're just down on PresiBot." He wiped sweat from his brow. "Boy, it's hot in here."

"Sorry, it's all the computers," said Arvind. "We've used up our October air conditioning quota."

"Apparently the voters don't want the nuclear codes in the hands of a crash-prone robot," said Kowalski, who in a pantsuit and heels was by far the best-dressed person in the room.

"That's not fair," said Ethan. "PresiBot is way better at complex decisions than at shaking hands."

"The opposite of regular politicians," said Arvind.

"Try explaining that to the voters," said Kowalski.

"PresiBot actually did pretty well in the debate, before the . . . accident," said Ethan.

"True," said Rossi. "Better than I expected."

"Practice makes perfect," said Arvind.

"Yeah, but those hundred million debates against Simulated Bull really broke the bank in cloud charges," said *Emma*.

"Maybe we can sell Simulated Bull to the real one's campaign as a backup," said Ethan. "We really need the revenue."

Arvind chuckled. "Where's Kristen, by the way?" he said. "Shouldn't she be here?" Kristen was KumbAI's simulation expert.

"I fired her," said Ethan. "She wanted to have a life, so I let her."

"Another one? No way," said Arvind.

"Sorry, anything less than total commitment doesn't cut it around here."

"I liked her," said Arvind. "Who's going to run all the simulations now?"

"Er . . . how about you?"

"Are you kidding? I may not have a life, but I'm not ready to die from overwork, either."

"Well, none of the others know the simulation code base, so if you don't do it, we're all dead."

Arvind sighed.

"We gotta do something to turn this campaign around," said Rossi.

"We just need more Presiheads," said Kowalski. Presiheads were PresiBot's most devoted fans, near-religious followers who thought humans were hopeless, AI the salvation, and PresiBot the messiah.

Rossi chuckled. "We're all maxed out on those, I think."

"They're great, though," said Kowalski. "Did you see? There's a conspiracy theory going round on Happinet that PresiBot was sabotaged."

"Perfect!" said Emma. "How do we feed it?"

"Good question," said Kowalski.

"Er . . . let's maybe not do that," said Arvind.

"What then?" said Kowalski.

They were silent for a moment.

"On the bright side, there are still a lot of undecideds," said Rossi.

"Who are they?" Emma asked.

"Mostly under-30s," said Rossi. "They're not sold on PresiBot, but having an AI president doesn't faze them, unlike older types. And that's a start."

"But they don't vote," said Emma.

"Nope."

"So the older generation is still solidly behind Raging Bull?" she asked.

"Now more than ever."

"How can people even be contemplating voting for him?" Arvind burst out. "PresiBot is obviously so much better."

Rossi chuckled. "They're not as smart as you," he said.

"We gotta get those under-30s to the polls," said Ethan.

"What are their pain points? And how do we ballotize them?"

Rossi shrugged.

"The usual," he said. "No jobs. Housing too expensive. Anxiety."

"PresiBot can fix all that," said Ethan.

"Yeah, maybe, but their belief that PresiBot can deliver anything just took a big hit."

"If only they knew how awesome PresiBot really is," said Arvind.

"What's amazing is that anyone is willing to vote for a candidate that can't even stand up," Kowalski said.

"No, people can tell the difference between the robot body and the actual AI," said Arvind. "The brain is what counts."

"I don't think so," said Kowalski. "In fact, the whole point of having a body is that voters subconsciously see PresiBot as more of a normal candidate."

"Normal candidates are overrated," said Arvind.

"But they win elections," said Kowalski. "Machines don't."

"We should have stuck with a virtual avatar," said Emma. "None of this robotics crap to deal with."

"You saw the polls," said Ethan. "People are much more likely to vote for a candidate with a body."

"It's not even clear a disembodied AI would pass the *Blinky v. U.S.* test," said Rossi.

"And anyway, the virtual avatar would have fallen down the same way in a realistic virtual auditorium," said Ethan.

"How could PresiBot fall down like that?" blurted out Kowalski. "I'm sorry. Never m—"

"Edge case," Ethan shrugged. "Leaning down from a stage, guy shaking its hand far too hard. No training data for that."

"Whatever," Arvind said. "We're not responsible for that pile of carbon fiber. Our product is IntelliProp."

"Fat lot of good that'll do us now," said Emma.

"Well, at least PresiBot doesn't lose his temper all the time, like Raging Bull," said Ethan.

"Hey, that's an angle we could exploit," said Arvind. "Contrast PresiBot's rationality with Raging Bull's irrationality. Emphasize the soundness of its mind over the . . . er . . . unreliability of its body."

"Nah," said Kowalski. "We just need to divert attention from the whole thing, and the sooner the better."

Rossi nodded. "Bottom line, we need to erase the image of PresiBot in pieces from people's heads," he said, his gaze involuntarily falling on the robot, "or we're toast."

"The right ad would do it," said Kowalski.

"Like what?" said Ethan.

"I dunno," said Kowalski. "Something projecting strength, and . . . indestructibility."

"OK, PresiBot as superhero," said Ethan. "Flying around, zapping bad guys, stuff like that. A robot can do things a human can't. We can play on that."

"But that's not relatable," said Kowalski.

"I think we gave up on relatable when we picked a computer as the candidate," said Rossi.

"I think the more superhuman PresiBot seems, the better," said Ethan.

"Do we have any actual data on this?" said Arvind. "Do voters like superhuman presidents over relatable ones?"

"What data?" said Emma. "From previous superhuman presidents?" They chuckled. "Seriously, though, I can find some proxies and run a model. And we can do a flash poll on Happinet."

"Yeah . . ." said Ethan. "People might say they don't like a super-human president, but deep down they do."

"I'm meeting with the RNC folks in DC tomorrow," said Rossi. "What do I tell them?"

"Let's do the superhero ad," said Ethan. "Linda, how quickly can you turn it around?"

"Maybe a *couple days,*" *she said,* "*if it's all computer-*generated."

"OK," said Rossi. "What else?"

"I think at a minimum we also need to make some changes to PresiBot's stump speech," said Kowalski.

"It doesn't quite look ready to go back on the stump," said Rossi, with a nod toward the severed head.

"I just called Oakland Robotics," said Arvind. "They say they'll have it fixed in a week."

"A week?" said Rossi. "We have less than a month left in the campaign. Can't they speed that up?"

"They need to order some parts from China," said Arvind.

Rossi shook his head in disbelief. "Imagine if the media got a hold of that," he said.

"Why don't you have a backup?" said Kowalski.

"Ha. Can't afford it," said Ethan. "Do you have any idea how much this one cost?"

"Ask Ungall for money. I dunno."

"Ungall is not an investor in KumbAI. We have to be very careful what money we take from whom. And we don't want to dilute our ownership of the company any more. We've almost lost majority control as it is."

"Besides, it's too late now," said Arvind. "It's a custom-made robot. There's no time to make another one."

"What we need is a new event in the campaign," said Ethan. "Something that will put the spotlight on Raging Bull until PresiBot is up and running again. Like a scandal that goes viral on Happinet. Has Fred found anything?" Fred was a scuzzy consultant they had hired to do oppo research on Raging Bull.

Rossi shook his head. "After his invasion stunt, Raging Bull is immune to scandal," he said. "Nothing compares."

"Big scandals can start from tiny things," said Ethan. "If the conditions are right."

"Yeah, maybe Dave Newald can arrange it for us," said Emma. "Isn't it included in Happinet Premium?"

Everyone chuckled. Newald was the founder and CEO of Happinet, and the world's richest man. Just then Ethan's phone rang.

"Excuse me a sec," he said, and went out into the corridor. "Hello?"

"Hi," said the voice on the other end. "This is Dave Newald."

"Yeah, right."

"No, seriously. Can we meet sometime soon? Like, in thirty minutes? I'm leaving tonight for a Senate hearing in DC."

"Er . . . sure."

"Great. I'm at the Flower. Bring Arvind Subramanian," said Newald, and hung up.

Ethan went back in.

"You'll never guess who that was," he said.

"Dave Newald!" said Arvind.

"Yep," said Ethan.

"Ha ha," said Arvind.

"I'm not kidding. You and I are meeting with him at the Happinet Flower in thirty."

"No way," said Emma.

"Way," said Ethan.

"What does he want?" Rossi asked.

"Guess we'll soon find out. By the way, has anyone seen the panic button?"

"You've lost the panic button?" said Arvind. "Seriously?"

"It's around here somewhere."

"What do you mean, panic button?" said Rossi.

"It's PresiBot's kill switch," said Arvind. "Every advanced AI has one, in case it goes haywire."

"Why haven't we told the public about this?" said Rossi.

"It would undermine PresiBot," said Ethan defensively.

"It would put to rest the notion that PresiBot could go rogue," said Rossi. "That would help."

"Nah, they'd still go on about it," said Ethan. "And then people would start asking who really controls PresiBot."

"Which is a good question, actually," said Rossi.

"Look, I'm the CEO. We made it. It's just not a good idea to focus on—"

"Well," said Emma, "right now no one controls it, because no one has the panic button." "Good job, Ethan," said Arvind.

"As I said, it's around here somewhere," Ethan said. "Don't panic."

"That's an ironic thing to say," Rossi said. "Can't we just ping it?"

Arvind shook his head. "Didn't implement that," he said.

"Why not?" asked Kowalski.

"Security hazard. Also, didn't have time."

They all started looking, poking under the desks, picking up empty pizza boxes.

"What's going on?" said one of the programmers.

"Don't worry about it," said Ethan.

"It's not on your desk?" said Emma.

"That's the first place I looked."

Suddenly Kowalski screamed.

"What's the matter?" said Ethan.

"A rat! I saw a rat! Over there!" she said, pointing to a hole in the baseboard.

"No fair," said Emma. "Why should it live here without paying its share of the rent?"

The rat darted out of an overturned wastebasket, across the floor and into PresiBot's broken neck.

"Oh no," said Kowalski. "Now what?"

"It's going to chew on the circuits," said Arvind in a panicky voice. "And then we'll really be screwed."

"Nah," said Rossi. "Maybe poke it with a broom?"

"Or put some cheese on the floor by the neck?" offered Kowalski.

"We need to leave soon," said Ethan, "or we'll be late. You guys deal with it."

"What about the panic button?" Emma asked.

"That too."

"Can't you just disconnect it and plug in another one?" Rossi asked.

"Hell no," said Ethan. "That would defeat the purpose."

"Even while it's, er, not functioning?"

"Particularly while it's not functioning. Otherwise anyone could just whack it and take control. Gotta go."

Ethan and Arvind sprinted out, while the others tried to dislodge the rat that had taken up residence in PresiBot's body.

3

YOU CAN SEE
THE WORLD FROM HERE

"Hurry up, we're late," said Ethan.

They were making their way down Market Street to the Happinet Flower, but kept stumbling on passed-out drug addicts and dodging discarded needles and piles of poop. Arvind, being less fit, was falling behind.

"Slow down, Ethan!" he heaved. "We're breathing too quickly! Don't you know that increases CO2 emissions?"

"They'll increase a lot more if we miss Newald and I throw a fit," Ethan shot back. "Move!"

Suddenly a junkie collapsed spasming on the pavement only feet from Arvind. He leaned down to help the man.

"Keep walking," said Ethan, without looking back. "We don't have the time."

"That guy needs help!"

"You want to help that one little guy, or you want to change the world? Focus!"

Ethan tripped on a sleeping hobo and fell face down on the pavement, inches from a used needle.

"What a fucking mess," he said irritably as he got up.

"Someone should do something about it. Like . . . sigh. If only I could clone myself."

"Hey, what are you so stressed about?" said the hobo, opening one eye. "Relax, man."

They resumed their sprint. Up ahead loomed the Happinet Flower, three hundred stories tall, wider than a city block, its stem of glass and steel blossoming at the top into seven vast petals, one for each of Happinet's divisions, in a 3-D rendition of the company's world-famous logo. Solar panels covered every inch of those petals, hungrily swallowing energy to help feed the even vaster underground data center on which the Flower stood. Fiber optic cables from the four corners of the world converged into that data center, the roots from which the Flower grew, yottabytes of data flowing through them every second like the bloodstream of an alien lifeform.

Ethan and Arvind made their way through Protest Plaza, the flagstone-paved square at the base of the Flower. A slim arch, emblazoned with the words "Happinet listens," spanned the plaza from side to side. A demonstration was in progress, as usual. They squeezed past a woman in a spike-studded leather jacket, army boots and tutu waving a sign saying "NEWALD IS SATAN" and another holding one end of a banner showing Happinet as an octopus with the Earth in its grip. The crowd chanted "Happinet is getting old/ We don't need your mind control." Finally they got to the front, but the security barrier stopped them.

"Darn," said Ethan.

"How do we get through?" said Arvind.

A Happinet employee in a light blue uniform was handing out bottled water to the demonstrators.

"Hey!" yelled Ethan. "Hey!"

The woman looked over at him.

"We're here to see someone!" yelled Ethan.

"What?" said the woman.

"We're here to see someone!" yelled Ethan again, cupping his hands around his mouth.

The woman came closer. "Hi," she said. "Would you like to schedule a protest?"

"No, we're here to see someone," said Ethan hoarsely.

"Oh, that's the other entrance," said the woman. "Go around the Flower. Would you like some water?"

"Shoot," said Ethan. They shoved their way back through the crowd, dodging insults and dirty looks, and sprinted to the other side of the building. The automatic sliding doors opened for them, and they headed to the row of desks at the other end of the atrium.

"Welcome to Happinet," said the receptionist. "Which position are you interviewing for?"

"We're not interviewing," said Ethan. "We're here to see Dave Newald."

She looked at him suspiciously. "Do you have an appointment?"

"What do you think?"

"I'm sorry. Please scan your ID here and read and sign the NDA here, then take a seat. Dave's XA will come get you shortly."

They sat down after doing the paperwork. The Flower's atrium was bright white and ten stories tall, with a hundred-foot-wide display spanning most of them. A video loop of the Flower's highlights filled the screen. "The Happinet

Tower was the tallest skyscraper in the world," said the narrator, "until the new Chinese Communist Party headquarters opened on Tiananmen Square in 2037." The display showed the Flower side by side with the Chinese tower, petals not quite as high as the giant Eye of Sauron atop it. "The bottom part of the Flower is taken up by the theme park, with levels celebrating each of Happinet's seven divisions." The video zoomed into the first level and swirled through the massive carousel occupying it. "The first level is Pride, where everything revolves around you. Jump from circle to circle until you're at the center, or go straight there if you're a Happinet Influencer of the Week. Next comes Envy, with rides inspired by our other social media properties, from MirrorWall to GossipTown. Let it all out on the Wrath Level! Visit the Happinews studio, then smash the newsmakers to pieces at Opinionation Live—aargh! Then on to Sloth and entertainment galore: arcades, movieplex, nonstop live shows at the Happistream Arena—enough to exhaust anyone! When you recover, take the escalator to Greed, where our legendary StonkMadness rollercoaster is located, in honor of Moneynet—one app for all your financial needs. Hungry for a break? The Gluttony Level has restaurants for all tastes, at all of which you can order using GoGoGourmet. And the Lust Level, for adults only, is your dating mecca: bars, clubs, nightly megaparties, and more. Tap on PheroMoan Match and find compatible singles right there. The next section of the Flower houses—"

"Hi," said a bright-looking young man, "are you the KumbAI guys?"

"Yes," said Ethan, getting up.

"Dave is expecting you. I'm Liam, his XA. Please follow me."

They passed through the security gates and headed to the elevators. Liam pushed the buttons for the three-hundredth floor, and they waited. The doors slid open, and they got in.

Ethan looked absently at the ceiling. An instrumental version of "Do You Know the Way to San Jose" emanated from the speakers. It reminded him of his father, who had been a serial entrepreneur in Los Angeles before moving to Silicon Valley at the height of the social media boom in the 2010s. The family had moved back to LA after all his ventures there had failed.

The elevator stopped on the 217th floor and two smartly dressed women got in.

"What are you doing this weekend?" said one to the other.

"I'm going to a white guilt retreat in Tahoe. What about you?"

"Dunno. Probably just kick back. Or maybe we'll go to a concert, or a protest."

"Which one?"

"Save the Penguins. They're so cute."

"Now there's an intractable problem."

"That way we'll always be able to protest about it."

"Yeah." Pause. "Don't you miss our young protester days?"

Sigh. "Those *were* the days."

The elevator stopped and the two women got out.

"Who was that?" said Ethan.

"Eve Adams," said Liam. "Our Token Female Officer."

"Ah. What does she do?"

"Nothing. She's just paid to be our TFO."

"How did you pick her?"

"She won the Random Woman in Tech Award."

"What's that?"

"It's given every year to a random woman in tech, just for putting up with everything that women in tech have to put up with."

"I see."

They arrived on the 300th floor, and Liam knocked on Newald's door. The man who opened it at first seemed like a teenager, lanky and freckled, but his thinning red hair, hard eyes, and early wrinkles soon gave away his real age of late thirties. He wore shorts, cross-training shoes, and a sweaty tank top that revealed surprisingly beefy arms.

"Hi, I'm Dave Newald," he said. "Come on in."

They were in a vast space surrounded by floor-to-ceiling windows, with an odd assortment of office furniture and gym equipment spread around the hardwood floor.

"I merged my office and my gym," Newald explained. "It's more efficient. Also, my thoughts flow better when I'm flexing my muscles." He picked up a pair of dumbbells. "I hope you don't mind if I continue working out while we talk."

"No, of course not," said Ethan.

"Check out the view," said Newald, doing bicep curls with the dumbbells.

Ethan stepped to the window and immediately stepped back, overcome by vertigo. They seemed to float in mid-air, separate from the world. Far below, San Francisco was flat and small in the sun's glare, traffic all but invisible.

The Golden Gate Dam, where the bridge used to be, was like a discarded drinking straw they could have inadvertently stepped on. A long line of ships waited to make the nine-inch descent through the locks. Beyond it, the mirror-smooth sea from whose rise the bay was now protected stretched impassively to the horizon.

"You know what's best about working at Happinet?" asked Newald.

Ethan shook his head.

"You can see the world from here," said Newald.

"Ah," said Ethan.

"Look at the people down there," said Newald.

Ethan squinted. "I can't make them out," he said.

"Exactly," said Newald. "People are pixels. When you just go about your daily life, surrounded by them, you miss the picture for the pixels. But when you start to work at Happinet, you finally see the whole."

"How's that?"

"The neurosniffer. When I invented it, I thought it would be an unprecedented window into the individual's emotional state. Think of it: one device, capable of reading—every moment—every molecule you release into the air, every pheromone, things you didn't even know were there, everything. Back then it was a big clunky machine, so using it on one person at a time was all I could do."

He put down the dumbbells and started pedaling on a stationary bike.

"But when we finally got it all down to a single chip and a single sensor you could pack into a cell phone, everything changed. One neurosniffer really is just one pixel, and what matters is the waves and troughs you can see moving through society, colliding, setting off bigger waves, without end. Bliss. Anger. Fear. Anger evoking fear. Husbands fighting with their wives when they get home from a football game their team lost. The impulse buying when the weather is nice. And then you can channel those currents. A push here, a nudge there, and a product that would be a failure turns into a runaway success. That's the joy of Happinet."

He stopped pedaling.

"Have you seen the control room? Here, let me show you."

He motioned them to the elevator, and they went down a floor, emerging into what looked like an indoor amphitheater with row after row of people intently focused on computer screens, and a continuous crackle of keystrokes and mouse clicks.

"Welcome to the social traffic control tower of the world," said Newald.

Wow, thought Ethan. *KumbAI will be this big one day.*

"Look," said Newald, sitting down at a free workstation. Ethan and Arvind huddled around him.

"Here's the dashboard for some random dude in Indiana."

A name at the top: Nathan Cameron. A row of meters, rising and falling, each labeled with a different emotion. Under it, a row of buttons. Across the bottom, a variety of information on autoscroll.

"Looks like he's enjoying a nice beer at the Flathill Pub in the Bloomington Mall. He's feeling pretty relaxed right now, but let's push the fear button," Newald said, clicking on it.

After a few seconds the fear meter started rising.

"Wow," said Arvind. "How'd you do that?"

"Neural Control—our system—chooses what to put in his feed to jack up the chosen emotion, moment by moment, from all the content available in the world."

But now the fear meter was falling and anger was rising, past the green bars and into the yellow, red, flashing— Suddenly all the bars dropped to zero.

"What happened?"

"Loss of signal," said Newald a little sheepishly. "Looks like dude just smashed his phone. We probably, heh, overstimulated him a little bit there."

"How did that— How did fear turn into anger?"

"Lots of ways that can happen. But here's my point. Who gives a shit about this one dude? Let's zoom out."

He pulled up another screen.

"We can slice the population any way we want, and show a dashboard for the aggregate. Here, let's do . . . everyone at this mall, male, 21 to 39."

He moved some sliders and clicked a few boxes.

"And let's say business at the Flathill Pub is kinda slow and they just sent us a winning bid for this demographic, so we want to make all those young men a little thirsty."

He scrolled left to reveal more meters and buttons and clicked one of them. Then he pulled up another screen, with the title "Flathill Pub, Bloomington, IN" at the top and several graphs.

"And here's the receipts from the Flathill, dollars by time. In thirty minutes or so we'll see this sloping up, showing the early Christmas gift we just sent them. Neat, huh?"

"But how many people will actually buy a beer or whatever because of what you did?" asked Arvind.

"Only a fraction, but that's plenty."

"What if it doesn't work?"

"Advertisers never lose money with us. If they share their revenue data and they didn't make what they expected, we refund them the excess bid. They love it. That's why we've grown so fast. Let's go back upstairs."

They headed back to the elevators, noticing for the first time the wraparound screen above them showing a live satellite world map with time zones, clouds over the Pacific, America plunging into darkness.

"Good evening, Happinerds," said a voice from the PA. "Dinner is now served in the cafeteria."

Everyone in the control room continued to work.

"And the Federal Technology Commission lets you do all this?" Ethan asked.

"Why not?" Newald said. "It's with the users' full consent."

"Ah."

"You don't believe me? There's a sentence in paragraph 500 and something of the Terms of Service that specifically let us . . . emotionally interact with the user, I believe is the wording."

Ethan nodded dubiously.

They emerged back in Newald's office. Down below, a blanket of clouds was coming in from the ocean, gleaming in the evening light.

Newald sighed. "It's not easy, you know, being in charge of humanity. People depend on us for their happiness."

He started doing bench presses. "Did you know we're the fastest-growing company in history?" he said in between pushes. "Nine years ago we didn't even exist, and now we're almost half the Nasdaq." Push. "Once you have something like the neurosniffer, nothing can stand in your way." Push. "Predicting and manipulating emotions is the linchpin of the world economy."

Newald got up, jumped on a treadmill, and jacked the incline up to 40 percent.

"How many psychologists and, er, sociologists work at Happinet?" Arvind asked.

"We have no use for those people," Newald heaved. "*Or their bullshit theories.*" *He paused for breath.* "*You can* learn more from one day of Happinet data than from the entire history of social science."

"But how do you predict the effect of different interventions, then?"

"I could tell you, but then I'd have to kill you, heh heh. But no, seriously, it's nothing but a big Kalman filter. Like forecasting the weather inside your brain."

He stopped the treadmill.

"Emotions are just numbers. They can be measured and tweaked like anything else."

The sun was fast approaching the horizon. The shadow of the Happinet Flower stretched across the bay to Oakland, the petals creeping up the hills like a giant alien spider, reaching for the darkness in the East until they merged with it.

"But enough small talk," said Newald. "Here's why I wanted to meet." He turned his hard eyes on Ethan. "Your campaign is on its last legs."

"Oh, I wouldn't say that."

"Your poll numbers are cratering. Any more and you'll have to rename your AI CraterBot."

"Ha ha. And your point is?"

"I want to save you."

"How?"

"By putting Happinet to work for PresiBot."

"Go on."

"With our data and influence, and Neural Control on your side, PresiBot will be back in contention."

"What's the catch?"

"There is no catch."

"Then why would you do this?"

"Let's just say I don't think dissolving the United States is in Americans' best interests. Or Happinet's, for that matter. Also, it wouldn't hurt to have a friend in the White House, for a change."

"Sounds great. Where do we start?"

"By me acquiring you."

"Huh?"

"Obviously, Happinet has to acquire KumbAI before we can do anything else."

"Why?"

"Otherwise it's an unacceptable risk for us. Would you do it if you were me?"

"Why not? I'd say acquiring us is the bigger risk. People already think you have way too much power. When they find out you've bought PresiBot, not even Neural Control can save us from the tsunami that will follow."

"But I'm not buying PresiBot, I'm buying KumbAI, which as PresiBot well explained in yesterday's debate, are two different things."

"Cut the crap."

"The acquisition would have to remain secret until after the election, of course."

"Ah. You think you can pull that off?"

"You tell me. Can I trust you on this?"

"Of course you can. But is all this even legal?"

"It'll be challenged, I'm sure. But Pierre de Mensonge, our general counsel, thinks we'll prevail in the end, which is good enough for me. So let's—"

"But we haven't agreed to be acquired."

"What choice do you have?"

Ethan hesitated for a moment. "Just for kicks, how much would you pay?"

"Three hundred and fifty million, half in stock."

"You're kidding."

"Huh? You think you're not worth that much?"

"Of course not. We're worth way more."

"Based on what?"

"We have the most advanced AI technology in the world. Didn't you hear? We've solved AI with the IntelliProp algorithm."

Newald burst out laughing. "Come on," he said. "Save that for the media."

"Arvind, what do you say?"

"Er . . . whether or not we've solved AI, we certainly have highly advanced algorithms that would be very useful to Happinet."

"So when did you make more progress in AI than my sixty thousand researchers?" said Newald. "In grad school?

Or in the little over a year your startup has been around?"

"IntelliProp is a major breakthrough, believe it or not," said Arvind sniffily. "And we own it."

"OK, OK, I don't deny you have some potentially valuable IP. But that's already factored into the valuation."

"How come it's so low, then?" said Ethan. "The acquihire value alone is more than you're offering."

"How so?"

"Every one of our guys is an AI genius. They deserve a lot more than thirty million per head."

Newald pulled up some info on his laptop. "I don't think so. Anton Klubok's PhD is in string theory. Wang Hunluan, Cody Kim and Mort Fuldork don't even have PhDs. Apparently all they did was take an online data science class."

"Wow, you're old school. Do you know how many GitHub stars Cody has? And Hunluan?"

"Look, none of this really matters. Even if you have some great IP—big if—and a top-notch crew, your net value is still negative. I'm offering three fifty just to make you and your investors feel good."

Ethan could feel the anger rising within him, but he saw Arvind give him a worried look and managed to control himself.

"Why is our net value negative?" he asked.

Newald started practicing karate moves. "PresiBot is a huge liability," he said. "You're going to lose the election by a landslide, be a butt of ridicule, and probably go bust shortly after. See what I mean?"

Ethan wanted to say something, but couldn't think of anything.

"On the other hand, with us you'll win, PresiBot will be hailed as a stroke of genius, and every organization will want one like it. So you're right—KumbAI is probably worth tens of billions, at least, but only if we buy you."

"So split those tens of billions with us! It's only fair!"

"That ain't how it works, buddy." Newald raised his foot as if for a karate kick. "You have two choices," he said, heel pointed squarely at Ethan's face. "I will acquihire you or I will destroy you. Which will it be?"

"You're wrong! You're wrong! You need us to win, or the United States is kaput. And then what will you do? How would you like Raging Bull breathing down you neck?"

"Oh, I have other ways of dealing with Raging Bull," said Newald darkly, shadowboxing.

"Meaning what?"

"That's above your pay grade, buddy."

"Fine. But there's another problem. If you buy us for three fifty, we're damaged goods. It'll tell everyone that you don't really believe in us, and then what?"

"Oh, no problem there. We can set the nominal acquisition price in the billions, by making most of it contingent on performance targets you'll never meet. No one reads the fine print. Besides, the media loves a good story of Happinet massively overpaying for some customer-free startup."

"I still think you should take a closer look at our technology before deciding on the offer," said Arvind.

"But we don't have time."

"It needn't take long."

Newald thought for a moment, absent-mindedly doing foot sweeps.

"OK," he said finally. "I'll send Mike Granite over tomorrow morning." Granite was Happinet's CTO. "Does that work for you?"

"Sure."

"Great. And now I have to scram. We can talk on the way to the roof."

He started walking to the elevator, and Ethan and Arvind followed him.

"So, just out of curiosity, which division would we be in?" said Arvind while they waited for the elevator.

"Politics is under Wrath, so that would seem to be the natural home for you," said Newald.

"But politics is just one application for us," said Ethan. "A demo."

"OK, so what do you suggest?"

"We should be our own division."

"Are you kidding me? All twelve of you?"

"Thirteen," said Arvind.

"That's just the start," said Ethan. "We'll be at least a few thousand by the time—"

"I thought you had solved AI, making human labor unnecessary."

"Well, that's not how it works. We need systems engineers, data wranglers, labelers—"

"We've got ten million labelers in India alone. That enough for you?"

"OK, fine. I still think AI is a crosscutting technology that—"

"Now you're telling me how to run Happinet?"

"Fine. How about Pride, then?"

"Why Pride?"

"Well, since all the others flow from it. You know."

"Ah. I can certainly see how you personally would fit very well in there."

"Er...how about Sloth?" said Arvind. "It's the most varied."

Newald thought for a moment.

"Yeah," he said finally. "It's certainly where I throw all the odds and ends. Where is that elevator?"

A few moments later, the elevator arrived and they got on.

"Congressional posturings, I mean hearings, are so boring," said Newald with a sigh.

"What's it like?" asked Arvind.

"Talking to senators is easy, provided you remember two things. Number one, they know exactly zero about the tech industry, and have no interest in learning. The sole purpose of their questions is to preen for their constituents. Number two, they have the biggest fucking egos you've ever seen, because We the People, so you'd better be very humble." He sighed. "The only real problem with hearings is that the whole fucking mediasphere is watching for something to pounce on."

They emerged onto the helipad, in between two of the Flower's gigantic petals. Liam and an efficient-looking young woman were waiting by the helicopter.

"Gentlemen, have a pleasant evening, and don't expect me to raise the offer," said Newald. "After Mike does his due diligence and we get back to you, we'll need an answer in 24 hours."

Newald and Liam got into the helicopter and it took off into the night sky.

"I'll accompany you down," said the woman.

Ethan noticed a low roar behind them and turned around. "What is this?"

"Oh, it's the data center's cooling system," she said.

"Way up here?"

"Yeah, the Flower is like a giant chimney. A hundred-foot-wide fan at the bottom sucks the hot air from the data center, and it blows into the atmosphere up here, leaving the city below undisturbed."

"Wow," said Arvind. "That fan must really be something."

"Yep. Happinet is a leader in green tech, and this building is our showcase."

4

LORDS OF THE VALLEY

"So . . . what do you think?" said Arvind.

They had stopped to grab something to eat at TechBurger, and were waiting for their meals to 3D-print.

"What do I think of what?" said Ethan.

"The offer."

"No way in hell we're selling KumbAI for 350 million. It's insulting. We've solved AI. Add a couple zeros, and it's still short."

"We just need to persuade Newald of that."

"Or Granite, more to the point. You think you can do that?"

"Ah . . . Well, to be honest . . ."

"What?"

"You know. Maybe intelligence propagation does solve AI, but we don't have the experimental proof yet."

"PresiBot is the proof."

Arvind shook his head. "Granite will see right through that."

"How do we convince him, then?"

"The potential," said Arvind, squirming a little. "It's all about the potential. Once we scale it up some more."

Ethan looked at him for a moment.

"Sure," he said. "We've got potential up the wazoo. Hell, we've got you."

"Thanks, but that won't get us to a multibillion-dollar valuation."

"You can't convince Granite you're a multibillion-dollar genius?"

Arvind chuckled. "You're the expert at convincing people," he said. "Any tips?"

"No, just act like you're me."

"Should've thought of that. Guess I'm low on genius today."

They got their burgers and sat down to eat.

"You know, there are many advantages to becoming part of Happinet," said Arvind.

"Like taking orders from Newald?"

"More resources. Then we can really focus on the research."

"I know. But that's not a reason to sell ourselves short."

"I'm more worried about something else."

"What's that?"

"Putting PresiBot in Newald's hands. Makes me a little queasy."

"But it won't be—"

"Yeah, yeah."

"In any case, we're not selling. Not for 350."

"We need to at least talk with Steve Blaugen."

Blaugen was a senior partner at Gold Rush Ventures, their Series A lead investor, and a member of KumbAI's board of directors.

"Sure," said Ethan, and dialed Blaugen on his phone.

"Hello?" said a voice on the other end.

"Steve? This is Ethan."

"Hey. What's up? You've run out of money?"

"Any day now."

"No kidding."

"But that's not what I'm calling about."

"Tell me, then."

"Happinet wants to acquire us."

There was a pause on the other end of the line.

"Really. How much?" said Blaugen finally.

"350 million."

"Not bad."

"Not bad? It's ridiculous."

"Well—"

"And he wants an answer by tomorrow. We need to talk ASAP."

Another pause.

"I'm, er, kinda busy right now, but OK. I'm at Lords of the Valley. Stop by."

"You mean the dance club?"

"Yep. You know where it is?"

"Er—"

"Folsom, near Furniture Palace." said Blaugen, and hung up.

Twenty minutes later they were at the club.

"We're with Steve Blaugen," said Ethan to the doorman.

The doorman nodded. "He's in the Sand Hill Room. All the way in the back, door on the left."

Ethan and Arvind made their way through the crowd.

The strobe-lit dance floor was a cubist painting of flesh and fabric. A line of girls in skimpy dresses waited by the door of the Sand Hill Room. Ethan knocked, but the sound was completely drowned by the thumping retro-techno music.

"Hey, don't cut in line," said the first girl.

Ethan gave her a cutting look. He found a doorbell and rang. After a few moments, Blaugen opened it. He was a very tall, muscular man in his mid-forties, with sandy hair and gray eyes. He wore black jeans and a black silk shirt.

"Oh hey, come on in," he said. "Make yourselves comfortable."

The room had red damask velvet-covered walls and a small stage where a slender, dark-haired girl was going through a striptease routine. A dozen of Blaugen's friends sat on couches around the stage or chatted standing up.

"What's this?" said Ethan.

"I'm auditioning dancers for my birthday party next month," said Blaugen. "It's going to be the bash of the century."

"Cool," said Ethan. Arvind nodded awkwardly.

"The party's theme is 'VC rules'," said Blaugen, catching a G-string that the girl threw his way. "The girls are like startups. Every funding round is a piece of clothing they take off. And when they're naked, I fuck them."

Ethan chuckled. "Makes sense."

"That's why they have to be lean."

"And able to pivot."

"There you go."

"It's OK, Arvind," said Ethan with a sideways glance. "No need to blush." Arvind turned away, shaking his head.

Blaugen chuckled. The girl was now waiting for a signal from him.

"Next," he said.

The girl gathered her belongings, mumbling something about getting back to Fresno before her sitter took off, and slunk out. Another one came in, this one blonde and also slender.

"OK, pitch yourself to me," said Blaugen.

"Huh?" said the girl.

"Why should I fund, I mean hire you?"

The girl looked at him for a moment. "Because, er, I'm gorgeous?"

"Sure, but can you execute?"

"Watch me," she said, stepping onto the stage.

A waitress approached Ethan and Arvind and asked them what they wanted to drink.

"Tequila on the rocks," said Ethan.

"Diet Coke," said Arvind, looking at his shoes.

The waitress nodded and went to get the drinks.

"So," said Blaugen.

"We're not selling," said Ethan.

"Why not? You have a better plan?"

"We win the election and become a trillion-dollar company."

"Not gonna happen."

"Four weeks is a long time in politics," said Ethan.

"Indeed, longer than you have money for. But with a cash injection from Happinet—"

"We don't need Happinet. All we need is maybe fifty million. Between you and Tricorn—"

Blaugen shook his head. "Fifty's not even close to enough."

"But donors—"

"Donors give money to candidates they think will win. They're probably busy buttering up Mr. Raging Bullshit right now."

"Small donors."

"Not enough time, unless something happens."

"Let's make something happen."

"Like what?"

"We're working on it."

Blaugen sighed. "Is that all you got?"

"I— I dunno," Ethan stammered. "It's just—"

"Listen to me, Mr. Hotshot," said Blaugen. "Happinet's offer is a gift from the gods. Let's just concentrate on jacking it up. What do they want?"

"Arvind and I still own 55 percent of KumbAI, and we won't sell."

"Then you'll go broke before the week is over."

"Not if—"

"You won't get a penny from Gold Rush, or Tricorn, or anyone I know."

"There's lots of other investors."

"But not enough time. Besides, once you go for the bottom feeders, you're bottom feed."

Ethan glared at Blaugen.

"Ethan—" said Arvind.

"Dammit!" shouted Ethan. "We're not selling!" The girl stopped in mid-routine and looked at him.

Ethan clenched his fists. Blaugen crossed his arms, looking down at the much shorter man. A few seconds that felt like an eternity passed.

"Fine," said Ethan.

Arvind let out a long breath. "How much do you think we can get from Happinet?" he asked Blaugen.

"Half a billion sounds perfectly feasible," said Blaugen, "if you sell them on intelligence propagation."

Arvind nodded.

"Now if you'll excuse me, gentlemen," said Blaugen, "I have some fucking to do."

The air in the teepee was thick with smoke from the sacred pipe. Naomi Jackson tried not to cough, but it was in vain. *Can we get this rigmarole over with and get on with the strategy meeting?* she thought, shifting uncomfortably under the weight of the star quilt Raging Bull had given her at the hunkapi where she'd been ceremonially welcome into his clan. *The whole Lakota thing has gone to his head. It's ridiculous.* The quilt was too stifling, and always left a pile of lint on her suit. To make it worse, her back was starting to hurt from sitting on the ground. *I need to pee,* she thought irritably.

"Hear us, Wakan Tanka," intoned the paper-white medicine man, gesturing with the pipe. "Help us to defeat the robot puppet and its masters!"

Jackson had run some wacky campaigns in her time, but none like this one. There was the candidate for governor of California who wanted to give a pink rubber ducky to everyone, but she seemed tame compared to Raging Bull. He reminded her of Donald Trump, the Republican president she had cut her teeth campaigning against twenty years earlier. *Even that jerk was tame compared to Raging Bull,* she thought. Every campaign manager's job starts with managing her candidate, but that didn't apply to Raging Bull. He could be contained, at best. A picture of Raging Bull smashing up a china shop formed in her mind, and made her shiver. *You gotta do what you gotta do,* she thought, clenching her teeth. *Let's get this guy to the finish line.*

The wichasa wakhan took a puff from the calumet and passed it to Raging Bull, who growled "Death to the colonists! Wakan Tanka! Exterminate them all!" with fiery eyes and then momentarily closed them to concentrate on imprinting this message into the smoke coming out of his nostrils.

The smoke rose lazily up to the Great Spirit, swirling, widening, some of it finding its way to the opening at the top of the teepee, but most of it just hanging around, enveloping Raging Bull and his lieutenants in a ghostly fog.

He looks like a bull, thought Jackson. Thick neck. Heavyset. Hair-trigger temper. *And the grandiose delusions—they keep getting worse. Aren't the Clozapine and Antilude working? What if the voters find out?*

Raging Bull passed her the calumet, and she pretended to take a long, meaningful puff, then passed it to Valerie White, her chief strategist, hoping no one would notice the lack of smoke coming out of her nose and mouth. Her coughing still got worse.

As the smoke dissipated, the wichasa wakhan recited something about Iktomi and the White Buffalo Calf Woman, and they were done.

"So what's this ad the colonists have been running?" Raging Bull asked.

"Here, let me show you," said Jackson, reaching for the remote and pointing it at the TV in the back of the teepee, under a red banner saying "Make America Go Away."

The ad started playing. PresiBot was under attack from all sides. Wham! Bang! Pow! A steady stream of villains came at it from left and right, each waiting for the previous one to be disposed of before lunging at PresiBot. One stuck a knife in its back, but the blade crumpled against PresiBot's *indestructible shell. Thugs with machine guns popped up* from manholes, ra-ta-ta-ta, but the bullets ricocheted harmlessly off PresiBot's shiny carbon-fiber limbs and the American flag on its chest. Cars careened toward it front and back, but PresiBot jumped and rolled over them, or just flung them away with bare hands. A bazooka blew a gaping hole in its right biceps, but the hole promptly closed itself. Missiles rained down on PresiBot from the sky, but before they hit their target the robot flew up on its rocket-powered feet, dodging and swatting them away with karate chops and kicks. One missile slammed head-on into PresiBot, blowing it to smithereens, pieces of shrapnel raining down on cars and houses. The end? No—after a moment of terrifying stillness, the pieces began crawling toward each other, melting together, taking shape, until PresiBot was one again and resumed its epic battle against the armies of evil. Whambangpow! The action sped up until PresiBot was a tornado, flying through the streets spewing thugs hither and thither, then high up into the air to intercept more incoming missiles, limbs glowing red. Finally the field was clear, and PresiBot landed majestically on the corpse-strewn street, bolt upright like a reusable rocket returning to Earth, arms folded, the camera angled up at it in awe.

"PresiBot is indestructible," said a deep, resonant voice-over. "And so is America."

Naomi Jackson pressed the off button on the remote and looked around the teepee.

"That's the most ridiculous ad I've ever seen," said Raging Bull, sitting cross-legged across from her. "We know that machine is a fucking cartoon, but why make it so obvious? All that's missing is a cape. I'm–PresiBot–and–I'm–here–to–whack–the–bad–guys!"

Naomi Jackson sighed. This was going to be a long slog.

"But it's working, though," said Valerie White. "PresiBot is already up almost ten percent in the polls."

"Big deal."

"Our support may seem large, but it's soft," said White. "Many of our voters aren't on board with our agenda. We're incredibly lucky the GOP goofed by picking a machine as their candidate, of all things."

"The question is how best to take advantage of it," said Jackson.

"Why, keep pounding home that Machine PresiBot is a tool of the rich," said Raging Bull.

"Yeah, but that doesn't work very well against this ad," said White. "We need to counter it with something. And soon."

"I think they just did us a great favor," said Jackson. "This ad—this tack—is the mistake that will finish sinking their campaign."

"Oh? How so?"

"It plays beautifully into the narrative that PresiBot is the bringer of the Robopocalypse. All we have to do is put out an ad showing it turning those awesome powers of destruction against ordinary people. A vast swarm of PresiBots descends from the sky, killing everyone in sight, etc."

"Bullshit," said Raging Bull. "We all know that's not going to happen."

"That's not the point. Voters will respond to it. They'll be horrified. It plays into their fears of AI. PresiBot will never recover."

"You don't think it's over the top?" said White.

"It would have been, if PresiBot hadn't done us the favor of putting out this 'I'm a superhero' ad. At this point it's just the logical next step. What do you think, John?"

Raging Bull hesitated. "Well, we can do that, but the main point is still that PresiBot is Ungall's bitch," he said finally.

"PresiBot had a point in the debate, though. We can't have it both ways. They interfere with each other, and the result is no strong message comes through. Plutocracy or Robopocalypse: we have to choose."

"It's plutocracy, then."

"But this ad just gave us the perfect opportunity to run with Robopocalypse."

"So what? It's just an ad."

"The problem with plutocracy is that people have heard it all before. We always paint Republican candidates as shills for the rich. It barely registers. Robopocalypse gets a lot more attention."

"It's not new either. Hollywood has been hammering on

it for decades."

"And so laying the groundwork for us. Thanks, Hollywood! People are all primed to have nightmares about PresiBot. What more could we ask for?"

"I don't fucking like it. This campaign is about liberating America from the colonists once and for all. What's the Robopocalypse got to do with it?"

"It doesn't matter. It's what works. Talk of abolishing the USA makes a lot of people nervous. We need to tone it down. We've been over this before, but you seemed to forget it in the debate."

"Fuck that! Abolishing the USA is the rallying cry for our troops. Where would we be without it?"

"Our troops are not enough to win the election. We need regular voters, independents."

"But we're doing great with independents—that's what the polls show!"

"We got a big bump from PresiBot's decapitation, but that's already fading away."

"We're going to sweep away the entire rabble of colonists!" shouted Raging Bull, pounding on the floor. "Fat cats! Bribe takers! Bison killers! Tech bros!"

"Look, John, I can tell you, as a Black woman, that your antics are off-putting. Your 'Death to America!' shtick may play well with guilty white folks, but it won't get you any Black or Hispanic votes. And without those you're toast. We need less testosterone and more bread and butter."

"Blacks and Hispanics? Blacks and Hispanics? You don't have the right to tell me what to do! You don't belong here either!"

"What's the matter with you? Do we need to call Dr. Krapow?"

"No! I'm fine! Leave me alone!"

"Then get a grip on yourself."

"I. Will. Not. Pander. To—"

"Then you'll lose the election."

Raging Bull opened his mouth to yell, but then stopped.

"Fine," he grumbled. "You can have your Robopocalypse. But it better work."

Thank God, thought Jackson. Her back hurt. "OK, let's *talk about the ground game. We have—*"

"Can we go back to making war videos?" said one of Raging Bull's cronies, playing with his weapon. "This is so boring."

"It's how you win elections," said Jackson.

"Yeah, I'd rather just play kill-the-wasichu," said another mock warrior.

"That was good for getting attention," said Jackson tartly. "Now we need to get votes. That's how democracy works."

"Just wait until I'm president," said Raging Bull. "I'll show you what I do with democracy then."

Jackson and White looked at each other.

"Anyway," said Jackson. "We need to shore up our ground game. The average age of our supporters is 55, and old people don't knock on doors."

"We need more money to hire canvassers," said White.

"The problem is, John," said Jackson, "the unions don't like you, and you've pissed off all our big donors with your attitude."

"OK, we'll rob a bank," said Raging Bull.

"Excuse me?"

"No one will stop us, and seeing it on TV will energize the troops."

"But robbing a bank is a crime."

"So is gunning down colonists. All in a day's work."

"Yeah, but fake money doesn't buy things."

"I mean it. We'll rob a bank. For real."

White opened her mouth as if to say something, but then closed it again.

"We'll announce it on Happinet tonight," said Raging Bull.

"Alright!" said the first crony. "Some fun at last!"

Here we go again, thought Jackson.

She doggedly steered the meeting through several more hours of back-and-forth. When it was over, she grabbed her Hermès purse from the parquet floor, stood up with a grunt, attempted to straighten her St. John skirt suit, put her Prada shoes back on, and walked out of the teepee and into the Potomac Ballroom of the Glassman Hotel in Washington, DC. She hurried past the other teepees of Raging Bull's entourage and down the hall to the restroom, followed by White.

"You don't think this guy is a little cuckoo?" said White as they washed their hands.

"Yes, but he's useful," said Jackson. "And it was their turn to pick a candidate."

"Beats me why they picked him. Wouldn't a real Native American be better?"

"No real Native American would do the crap he does. Besides, he gives them hope."

"Maybe. It's just a little odd, that's all."

"Well, Napoleon wasn't French, and Hitler wasn't German."

"Hitler? Wow."

"I didn't mean— You know what I meant."

"But aren't you afraid of what he'll do if he's elected?"

"Come on, there's no way he can get his agenda through. What matters is we'll have a Democratic president."

"I don't know. Looks like we're on the way to big majorities in both houses. And the states—"

"Well, I'd rather have an Indigenous Federation run by us than a United States run by the GOP."

"But he's delusional," insisted White. "He really thinks he's a Lakota chief. This isn't going to end well."

"Posing as a Lakota chief works. That's what matters."

White shook her head. "I don't know."

"Come on, Val. John is actually a pretty good actor. People don't give him enough credit. Reagan played the cowboy. He plays the Native American. What's the difference?"

White grimaced. "He looked at my breasts," she said.

"Spare me," said Jackson, drying her hands.

"PresiBot wouldn't do that."

"See you tomorrow, Val," said Jackson, walking out of the restroom.

I need a drink, she thought.

She headed out of the hotel and took the subway to the Master of Margaritas, a pub popular with political operatives. Scanning the bar for a seat, she spotted Vince Rossi.

"Hey, what are you doing in DC?"

"Eh, you know. The usual."

"May I join you?"

Rossi hesitated for a moment, then shrugged. "Sure, why not? Sleeping with the enemy, and all that."

"I wasn't thinking of taking it quite that far."

"True, we're both married to politics."

"And she's a jealous spouse."

The Master of Margaritas was one of those old-fashioned pubs that still had a human bartender. Jackson ordered a Long Island iced tea and turned back to Rossi.

"Remember the Boyle campaign?"

"I beat you fair and square."

"For the last time ever."

"Hey, I have superpowers now."

Jackson burst out laughing, with an edge of nervousness.

The bartender brought her drink, and she downed it in one gulp.

"You know what I would do if I was you?" she said.

"Pray tell."

"Start a consultancy called Robopolitics."

"And . . . ?"

"When a party can't find a good candidate for a race, you rent them a robot."

"Wow, brilliant. The demand would be bottomless."

"Unlike this glass," Jackson said, looking at her empty drink. "Bartender! Another Long Island iced tea!"

"You look like you've had a rough day," Rossi said.

"Politics is rough."

Rossi nodded. "Who has the harder job, me or you?"

"Me, for sure."

"Why is that?"

"PresiBot doesn't throw temper tantrums, for one."

"But Raging Bull doesn't have bugs."

"Oh, he has plenty of those. And at least PresiBot stays

on message."

"You'd be surprised."

"Sometimes I wish I could just program Raging Bull, like you program PresiBot."

"Oh, we don't really program it. We just give it training data and . . . pray."

"Admit it, you like working with geeks, because deep down you're one."

"Trust me, I'm nowhere near them on the geek scale. I'm just a regular guy from Brooklyn who got into direct mar-keting and then politics."

"How does a regular guy from Brooklyn turn into a Republican?"

"Runs in the family," shrugged Rossi.

They ordered another round.

"So what will you do after this campaign is over?" asked Jackson.

"You mean after we've won? Be PresiBot's chief of staff."

Jackson chuckled. "But PresiBot doesn't need a chief of staff."

"Well, it needs a campaign manager."

"True."

"Because it's actually a lot harder than being the can-didate."

They both laughed. The bartender brought them their drinks and they quaffed them down.

"So where you staying?" asked Jackson.

"The Dupont Inn, down the street from here."

"Good place for a threesome."

"Hmm?"

"You, me and politics."

Rossi smiled and leaned over. Jackson stopped him, shaking her head. "Not in public, you wild and crazy man."

Rossi nodded and got the bill. "Boy, that's a lot of drinks we've had."

"And a lot fewer than we need. OK, let's go." She got up unsteadily. "Good thing your hotel is so close."

They headed out and down the street to the Dupont Inn.

5

HOW TO BE A GENIUS

Arvind and Mike Granite waited for a breakfast table at the Space Bar, the Garage's cramped cafeteria. Granite struck up a conversation with the man ahead of them in line.

"So what do you do?"

"We make shopping carts for the homeless."

"Ah."

"You know, to keep their things. Pretty spiffy. Mini-fridge and microwave included."

"And homeless people have enough money to buy them?"

"No, the city buys them. Much cheaper than shelters. It's going to take off like wildfire."

"Right. What's the name of the company?"

"Cordon Bleu Tech."

"Doesn't quite bring shopping carts to mind," said Arvind.

"That was the original name, before we pivoted to carts. We decided to keep it." He paused, looked at Arvind. "What about you, what do you make?"

"Presidents."

"Oh that's right, you're one of the KumbAI guys." He turned to Granite. "I feel like I also know you."

"This is Mike Granite," said Arvind.

"Wow. We have a living legend in the Garage today. To what do we owe—"

"Top secret," said Arvind. "You never saw us."

"Roger that."

There was a moment of awkward silence.

"Oh, there's my table," said the man. "Great to meet you, Mike."

When their turn came, they sat down and started to eat.

"I read your paper," said Granite, sipping his coffee.

"Which one?"

"The one on intelligence propagation."

"The first one?"

"I don't know. The one from the 2039 Conference on Novel Intelligent Processes and Systems. Subramanian and Jeffington."

"OK."

"So how does intelligence propagation solve AI?"

"It formalizes the brain as a massive nonzero-sum network game with convergence properties determined by the symmetries of the combined manifold of the state spaces, which becomes progressively more curved in the original representation, but progressively less in the—"

"Whoa whoa whoa. I'm just a systems guy, so you'll have to slow down and use less AI jargon."

"OK." Arvind thought for a moment. "The whole problem in AI is how to get complex behavior to self-organize from simple units like neurons or logic gates."

"That's starting from a very low level."

"Yes, but if you start with large preprogrammed

components, they're too rigid, and the system's intelligence is less than the sum of its parts. So you get nowhere. Intprop—intelligence propagation—tells you how to make the whole more than the sum of the parts, at every level. The result is an intelligence explosion."

"Sounds like magic."

"It's not, it's the result of the mutual bootstrapping theorem."

"I saw that in the paper, but I didn't follow."

"We lift each other up by each other's bootstraps. If you *give me some information that makes me smarter*, I now have more information than the sum of what I started with and you gave me, and by sharing that with you—"

"Why more?"

"Because the information made me smarter. Because of the epsilon in the theorem."

"What's that?"

"Epsilon is the amount by which the new information exceeds the old, at each step. It can be tiny, but it just has to be greater than zero—that's all it takes."

"Can you give me an example?"

"We fed billions of documents into PresiBot, but not passively. Each document has like a little brain built on top of it, initially very stupid, because it only knows what's in that one document and barely understands it. But then the mini-brains start exchanging information, and they get smarter. Sometimes your document helps me understand mine better, so I extract more information from it, so I can help you understand yours better. With only a few documents this doesn't get you very far, but with billions—it's amazing. The mini-brains coalesce into larger and larger brains, and PresiBot comes to life."

"Hum. That still sounds very handwavy. Not like something I could implement. And the pseudocode in the paper doesn't help much, either."

"Of course not. You can't just implement intprop from the pseudocode. Or rather, you could, but it won't work."

"Seriously?"

"Well, yeah, there's a lot of secret sauce, implementation details, black magic, whatever you wanna call it. That's what gets you the epsilon in the theorem."

"I thought the theorem gave you the epsilon."

"No, it only says that if there's an epsilon, there will be an intelligence explosion."

"Let me get this straight. The paper your company is allegedly based on doesn't actually tell you how to solve AI."

"Well, part of it."

"But not all."

Arvind shrugged.

"Whatever happened to reproducibility?"

"That's such a 20th century concept. Modern AI is too complex to be reproducible. Besides, if we put everything in the paper, what would be our competitive advantage as a company?"

"What's the point of writing the paper, then?"

Arvind shrugged. "It's kind of a . . . commercial, for the research, really."

"Yeah, but now that I've seen the commercial, I want to kick the tires before I buy the car."

"Sure, but I can't reveal any of our secrets to you."

"I signed the NDA."

"Good luck to us enforcing an NDA against your millions of lawyers."

Granite sighed. "So how are you going to optimize America, exactly? It's a big leap from intprop."

"Thanks to intprop, PresiBot knows America better than anyone or anything. Given each American's utility function, it can maximize the average utility of all Americans."

"And do you have each American's utility function?"

"Not yet. That's the next step."

"How are you going to acquire it?"

"Er . . . we haven't really started thinking about that part yet."

"So what have you actually built so far?"

"Just the demo."

"Aha. And what's the demo?"

"PresiBot."

"But PresiBot is just a glorified chatbot."

"So far. So far."

"Then how does it prove anything about intprop?"

"Look, PresiBot is basically the result of mining a ton of data and running it through intprop. Without intprop, PresiBot wouldn't know how to do anything."

"Sorry to be blunt, but I don't know if I can believe you."

"I can't show you the details of intprop, but I can show you what it can do. Like what happens in PresiBot's brain when it's talking."

"Fine. Show me."

They bused their trays and went down the corridor to KumbAI's office.

"So you were Jeffington's student?" said Granite.

"Yeah. Still am, in fact. We're only on leave from Stanford while we do the startup."

"So was intprop his idea?"

"No, I pretended to be working on what he wanted me to, and I only told him about intprop after it was working."

"You mean when you had PresiBot up and running?"

"No, there was no PresiBot then. PresiBot started later, as a joke."

"A joke?"

"Yeah, we were having dinner one day after the *Blinky v. United States* decision, and we got pretty drunk, or at least Ethan did. And I said, 'You know, an AI could run for president now.' And Ethan said, 'Yeah, let's do it.'"

"That was before KumbAI?"

"No, we'd already started it, but it wasn't going very well. We needed publicity. Too many AI startups. You need some way to stand out."

"Well, you got your publicity, all right."

"No kidding."

"How did you come up with the name KumbAI?"

Arvind shrugged. "Our first name was Shambhala Systems, but it sounded too much like Shambolic Systems. KumbAI has this nice sense of everything coming together and working in harmony, which is really the idea of intprop, or IntelliProp, as we rebranded it."

"Aha."

They went into the office. Arvind pulled up a chair for Granite, and they sat down at his workstation. Arvind pointed to the cube with blinking LEDs jammed into the space between his monitor and the next desk's.

"This is PresiBot's local brain," he said. "The body is, er, being repaired right now. And of course, for the heavy lifting it connects to the cloud."

Granite nodded.

"So ask it a question," said Arvind.

"It can hear?"

"No, but I'll type it in."

"Any question?"

"Sure," said Arvind, trying to look confident.

"How much should we pay for KumbAI?"

Arvind cursed to himself. *Why didn't I think of that?* He typed in the question, and a graph appeared on the monitor's screen, with each word as a node. The edges got thicker, and the nodes redder. "How" and "much" merged. But one node stayed pale and thin.

"See," said Arvind, "it doesn't know what 'we' refers to, so it's going to ask."

"Who is 'we'?" appeared across the bottom of the screen.

"Happinet," typed Arvind.

The nodes all coalesced into one big blob, which started pulsating and sending out tendrils, shrinking into the center of the screen as other blobs of all colors appeared, overlapping, changing shape and sending out new tendrils in turn.

"It's looking up info about Happinet," said Arvind, "and figuring out how it relates to KumbAI."

"What's with the pulsating rhythm?" asked Granite.

"Oh, that's just for fun."

"And the psychedelic colors?"

"Yeah, not sure about that."

"It's pretty cheesy."

Arvind shrugged.

"Looks like something you put together for your investors."

"Yeah," said Arvind sheepishly.

A few more seconds passed, then "Zero dollars" appeared on the screen. Arvind could feel his face burning red.

"Pretty smart," said Granite.

"Why zero?" typed Arvind.

"KumbAI's net present value is negative," said the display.

"What would make it positive?" typed Arvind.

"Winning the election," said the display.

"Won't Happinet help?"

"Yes, but the chances of winning are still minuscule. Not enough to make the NPV positive."

We're toast, thought Arvind. *Shoot.*

"Ask it 'What if intprop is a lot better than Happinet's current AI algorithms?'" said Granite.

Arvind typed in the question.

"Up to seven point four trillion dollars, depending on how bad the current algorithms are," said the display.

"Wow," said Arvind. "How bad are your current algorithms?"

"Pretty damn good," said Granite, coughing. "I was just trying to get some loose bounds."

"Actually," said Arvind, taking a deep breath, "after talking with Dave, I have a feeling they could be a lot better."

"Well, yeah, of course. But mostly our bottleneck is scaling, as always. Nothing burns cycles like AI. So PresiBot runs in real time on this—what is it?"

"It's a Cheetah 5.1. Yeah, the vision and motor control are onboard, but the learning, language processing and inference are still mostly cloud-based."

"Figures. You use our cloud?"

"Yeah, actually."

The back-and-forth continued for a while, with Granite asking Arvind how they maximized throughput to the cloud, how they ran the inference in real time, and more.

Finally Granite sat back. "OK, I'm good," he said.

"So what do you think?"

Granite smiled. "I don't think you've solved AI," he said.

Arvind's heart sank.

"But I'm impressed with how you've managed to integrate the Cheetah with our cloud in real time. We can certainly use people like you at Happinet." He paused. "You know, if the acquisition doesn't work out, you can always come work for us after—"

"After KumbAI is history?"

"I didn't say that."

"But that's what you were thinking."

"Just make sure your pigheaded CEO agrees to sell."

"OK, everyone, quiet down," said Ethan.

They had rented the Space Bar for an all-hands meeting. Ethan waited for the noise to die down.

"I have an announcement to make."

The silence was now total.

"We're being acquired by Happinet. Just closed the deal."

The room erupted into cries of excitement and celebration.

"How much? How much?" said several voices.

Ethan paused for a moment, for suspense and to conceal his bitterness.

"355 million."

"Yeah!" Fist pumping, high fives.

"Now, very important. Extremely important. The acquisition must be kept confidential until after the election. Everyone got that?"

Nods and yeahs.

"All right, everyone. Let's celebrate."

Pop, went a bottle of champagne. Glasses clinked, music pumped from the Space Bar's speakers, loud conversation filled the room.

Time to get drunk, thought Ethan.

"Don't sulk," said Arvind. "355 million is really not that bad, you know."

"This is all Steve Blaugen's fault."

"But now we have the means to beat Raging Bull."

Ethan nodded grudgingly, and wandered over to where Anton Klubok and Mort Fuldork were heatedly debating the coming of the Singularity.

"It's gonna be a least a decade," said Anton.

"Not if we have anything to do with it," said Mort.

"That's the spirit," said Ethan.

The party was now in full swing, and as the empty beer and wine bottles piled up the Singularity seemed to get nearer and nearer.

After a while Arvind snuck away to get some work done. Others started to leave as well, until only Ethan and Emma were left, splayed on the Space Bar's plastic chairs, still drinking.

"You did it! You're amazing!" Emma said.

"*We* did it," Ethan said. "We."

"You're too modest."

"Yeah, that's my biggest shortcoming," said Ethan, and they both laughed.

Ethan's glass was empty. Emma poured the last of a bottle of Chardonnay into it, then, with a giggle, opened *another and refilled hers.*

"We're rich now!" she marveled, glass in hand, in a drunken haze. Ethan nodded morosely.

An 80s power ballad emanated from the speakers. "Heaven isn't too far away / Closer to it every—"

"Let's dance!" said Emma, getting up unsteadily and tugging on Ethan's arm.

"Suuure," said Ethan, struggling to his feet. They held each other and swayed to the music. Emma hummed the song in his ear. Her arms tightened around him. He could feel her heart beating, and her cheek sliding past his. *I swear, she's going to kiss me,* he thought.

Suddenly they heard footsteps coming down the corridor, and awkwardly untangled themselves. Ethan had just sat back down when Arvind's face showed in the doorway.

"Time to go home, no?" Arvind said.

"Yeah, yeah," said Emma. "Bye, Ethan."

Ethan raised his glass to both of them.

Now he was alone with the empty wine glasses and dirty plates. He sighed. An image of him ringing the opening bell at the New York Stock Exchange flitted through his mind. *Next time, next time,* he thought.

Bright and early the next morning, Ethan rode the elevator to Newald's office with Liam. He had a throbbing headache, but was feeling better about the acquisition. *Arvind is right,* he thought. *With Happinet's money and power behind us, we'll whack Raging Bull in no time.*

Liam knocked, and Newald opened the door.

"You wanted to see me?" said Ethan.

"Yup."

Ethan moved to sit down.

"No need," said Newald. "This will be quick."

"OK."

"You're fired."

6

THE SINGULARITY IS HERE

Arvind arrived early for his meeting with Newald. The control room looked different, as if someone had decided to decorate it in the style of a Bollywood set. The workers at their desks were all shapely young women in ornate saris, and wore shiny metal headsets that made them look like the robot Maria from *Metropolis*.

"Good morning, PresiBot," said Newald, and snapped his fingers. Red LED lights went on in the headsets' front plates, and the girls all got up and formed a chorus line, singing:

> *Our hero has arrived!*
> *The battle will begi-i-in!*
> *To save the world from blight*
> *This battle he must wi-i-in!*

Newald made a dramatic gesture toward the roof elevator, whose doors opened, revealing a golden chariot pulled by a winged robot horse. The chorus line closed in around Arvind, nudging him toward the chariot. He got on hesitantly and the elevator doors closed.

Moments later he emerged on the roof. As the doors opened, an arrow grazed his shoulder and thwacked into the elevator wall behind. The horse bolted from the elevator, the jets in its wings coming to life, and the chariot took off from the Flower like a fighter from an aircraft carrier. Arvind ducked to dodge another arrow and looked up. Raging Bull, riding a winged horse with glowing red eyes, was bearing down on him fast. Arvind swerved to the right, and his hand instinctively grabbed the bow that hung from the side of the carriage. He aimed at Raging Bull, tracking him across the sky, and shot one, two, three arrows in quick succession.

The chorus line was now on the roof, morphing into a circle and then a flower shape with pulsating petals, singing:

Fly! Fly! Wondrous PresiBot! (Bot! Bot!)
Defender of Humanity and champion of Thought!
  (Thought! Thought!)
Kill! Kill! Kill the evil Bull! (Now! Now!)
With your magic arrows deliver us in full! (Wow! W—)

"ENGINE MALFUNCTION," flashed the display in the chariot's cockpit. The horse veered left and corkscrewed to the ground, dragging the chariot with it. The chariot slammed onto the asphalt and Arvind's neck onto the edge of the carriage, his head flying off, bouncing several times off the ground, and finally coming to rest on its side. Out of the corner of his static-filled eye, Arvind saw Raging Bull land and triumphantly walk toward him, tomahawk in hand. "No! Nooo!" he screamed.

"What's the matter?" said Emma sleepily.

Arvind opened his eyes.

"What—"

The late-morning sun slanted in through the blinds.

He grabbed his phone from the nightstand and checked the time.

"Shoot!" he said, jumping out of bed. "I slept through the alarm! I'm late for my meeting with Max Bozeau!"

"Hurry up, then," said Emma, turning over.

"What kind of startup CEO meets with his CTO at 8 a.m., anyway?"

"We're not a startup anymore, we're a subsidiary of Happinet."

"Still," said Arvind, getting dressed in a hurry. "If Ethan was still our CEO this wouldn't happen."

"I wish he was."

"Well, we tried," said Arvind with a sigh. He gave Emma a kiss and ran out the door, hair uncombed and T-shirt on backward.

When he arrived at the Garage, Bozeau was waiting for him at the conference table, his massive frame overflowing one of the rickety chairs, looking perilously like Humpty Dumpty before his fall.

"Can't wait to move to the Flower," said Bozeau.

"When will that happen?" said Arvind, sitting down.

"Well, the Flower's new underground floors are almost finished."

"We're going to be underground?"

"Sunlight is overrated, my friend."

"I don't know if I can function without sunlight."

"Don't you guys mostly work at night anyway?"

"We work twenty-four seven. Even while we're dreaming."

"Of course, of course. Anyway. Is PresiBot ready for tonight's big fundraiser?"

"The parts from China haven't arrived, but the Oakland Robotics guys say they can rig something that will hold together as long as PresiBot doesn't move."

"That's not very reassuring."

"The other option is to cancel it."

"No, not an option. What about the town hall in LA tomorrow?"

"That's where the big problem is."

"Uh-oh. What do you mean?"

"I've run a few million simulations of it, to train PresiBot."

"And?"

"They didn't go well."

"What do you mean?"

"Look, here's one."

Arvind turned his laptop toward Bozeau. It showed a rendering of PresiBot talking to a hundred or so people.

"People of Los Angeles!" said PresiBot. "I'm here to give you what you want, so tell me what you want and I'll do the optimization!"

"Lower taxes!"

"More government spending!"

"Great, great. I will lower taxes and increase government spending. Do you prefer skyrocketing debt or rampant inflation?"

"No! No skyrocketing debt! No rampant inflation!"

PresiBot computed for a while.

"We're going to need more resources," it said finally. "A

lot more resources. Starting with natural resources."

"No, save the Earth!"

"Annex Canada!"

"Yes, annex Canada and save the Earth. We'll need a bigger military—"

"Boo! The military is evil! Shrink the military!"

"Very well, I will instruct the National Guard to annex Canada. What if the Canadians object?"

"They won't object, they're nice people!"

"Challenge them to a game of football! If we win, they're ours!"

"What if they prefer hockey?"

"Fine!"

"What if they win?"

"Give them Alaska!"

"No, Antarctica!"

"Antarctica?"

"Yes, occupy Antarctica and rename it South Canada!"

"But what will Canada do with Antarctica?"

"Export bottled water and penguin meat!"

PresiBot computed for a while more.

"OK, what else do you want?"

"Rein in Happinet!"

"Dismember Happinet!"

"Dismember Dave Newald!"

Arvind stopped the simulation.

"It's all downhill from there," he said.

"What does this mean?" said Bozeau. "The people aren't being well modeled?"

"On the contrary, they're being all too well modeled."

"But look at what they're saying! It's nonsensical."

"It's all taken from real Happinet data. A mix of typical cases and edge cases, like real town halls. So overall it's representative."

"Representative? Annex Canada?"

"I guess people are wackier than we thought. The long tail is very long. But the point is, we're stuck. America can't be optimized."

"Why?"

"People want too many contradictory things."

"Well, sure, you can't make them all happy at the same time."

"No, each person wants too many contradictory things."

"Ha. Well, you have to make tradeoffs."

"But then they're not happy and we lose the election."

"How do you know?"

"That's what happens in every statistically significant batch of simulations."

"But Raging Bull can't work miracles, either."

"No, but he can lie."

"Well, we have to lie as well."

"Seriously? What are we running for, then?"

"To turn KumbAI into a non-loss-making unit of Happinet."

Arvind looked at him with disgust. "I thought we were going to disrupt politics."

"Oh, that's no longer a priority. Once we're in the black, maybe—"

"Are you kidding?"

"We need to monetize PresiBot."

"We have no time to think about that right now."

"KumbAI is not a startup anymore. We need to show some revenue."

"How?"

"We can turn it into a new persona for the Happinet smart speaker system, say. A significant segment of the population would probably enjoy ordering the president about," Bozeau said, looking pleased with himself.

Arvind open his mouth to say something, but then closed it. "OK," he said finally, "but first we have to win the election."

"Well, *what do you propose?*"

"I don't know. We're stuck."

The Friday night crowd at the Trouble Brewing Co. was in full swing. Ethan ordered another beer and went back to scrolling through his contact list for girls to call. Ashley? Brooke? Cecilia? Nah, nothing appealed. He tapped on the PheroMoan Match app and gazed distractedly at the TV above the bar.

"The Singularity is right on schedule," an extremely old man was saying on TV. "If a robot can be president, robots can do anything."

"Except not fall off a stage," said the interviewer.

"Well—"

"Who's that guy?" asked Ethan to the man next to him at the bar.

"You don't know? It's . . . whatsisname . . . that guy who's always saying the Singularity is near. Sooner or later he'll be right."

"If he lives long enough, which seems doubtful from the looks of him."

"Yeah, he's working on that. He has this longevity supplement business, or something."

"Sure, and I have a bridge in Brooklyn to sell you."

"Wow, you're quite the skeptic. What do you do?"

"Tech. CEO of a startup," lied Ethan.

"Exciting," say the man with a yawn. "What—?"

"You know, world domination."

The man chuckled. "I bet you're all a bunch of white guys," he said. "And Asians."

"No, we have a couple women."

"But no Blacks or Latinx, huh?"

"There aren't any in Silicon Valley," said Ethan with a shrug.

"That's what they all say."

"Look around you."

"True. Hey, I have an idea that will make us both rich."

"Tell me."

"I do a startup and you buy a billionth of it for a dollar. The startup is now worth a billion dollars, it's a unicorn, it's hot, and the money comes pouring in."

"And who pays the bail when we're arrested?"

"We don't know each other, so—"

"Have you considered a career in stand-up comedy?"

"No, I'm just drunk."

"Me too. Cheers."

"You don't look very happy."

"Oh man, you have no idea," said Ethan into his beer mug, and downed the rest of it in one gulp.

"Another round?" asked the robot bartender.

Ethan nodded sullenly.

"Startup not going well?" asked the man.

"No, we're actually getting acquired," said Ethan. *At least he didn't recognize me,* he thought.

"You should be celebrating, then."

Suddenly Ethan collapsed into sobs. "It's not fair! It's not fair! It's my company! I did everything—" He made a sweeping gesture, accidentally hitting the beer mug that the robot had just put down on the counter. The mug slid off the edge and exploded on the floor.

Ethan froze, looking at the shards. An image of his elbow pushing the panic button off his desk and into the wastebasket below flashed through his mind.

"Oh my God— Oh my God—"

"What?"

"I know what happened to the panic button."

"Huh?"

"Sorry, gotta go," said Ethan, and ran to the exit.

Ten minutes later he was banging on the Garage's door.

"All right, all right," said the janitor, opening the door. "I thought you didn't work here anymore."

"I—" said Ethan, and stopped to catch his breath. "I don't, but I forgot something. Can I go get it?"

"Well, if you don't have the key—"

Ethan barged past him, ran down the hall and started banging on KumbAI's door. Nothing. *Why is no one here?*

The janitor caught up with him.

"Look, mister—" he said.

Ethan kicked the door and flung himself at it until it started to crack.

"OK, OK," said the janitor. "Here," unlocking the door.

Ethan ran to his old desk and reached under for the wastebasket—empty.

"When did you empty this bin?" he nearly yelled at the janitor.

"Just now."

"And the last time before that?"

"Well, a week ago."

"Oh my God. Where is it?"

"Out front."

Ethan ran back outside. There—there was the trash can. He reached for the lid—but the trash can rose into the air, out of his reach. *What the heck?* He looked up. The trash can turned as it rose, in the grip of a garbage truck's robot arm. Its contents tumbled into the chute, and he caught a glimpse of the panic button on its way down.

"No— Noo—"

Ethan clambered onto the truck and tried to reach in— deeper—deeper—the garbage truck started up, and he fell in.

Oh God, I'm going to get compacted out of existence. A picture of himself squashed into a dripping cube of flesh flashed through his mind. The tailgate came down. It was now pitch black. He turned on his phone's flashlight and looked around. The compaction plate didn't seem to be moving yet. *Thank God.* He was sitting on a pile of trash. The panic button was nowhere to be seen. It must have fallen to the bottom. He started digging into the trash. Nothing. He burrowed into it like an oversize mole. The truck stopped, and he nearly dropped the phone. Light—trash tumbling in—darkness. *I'll find this freakin' panic button if it's the last thing I do.* He rummaged left and right, squinted, dug deeper. Still nothing. Finally, after what seemed like an eternity punctuated by stops and starts, he saw it. There—he reached for it, grasped it with a cry of victory, and dragged it through the garbage and into his back pocket. Now to get out. He tried to turn around in the garbage, but it was hard. The garbage was moving, crushing him. *Oh no.* The compactor had started. He clambered desperately up to the top of the garbage pile, and hit his head on the roof. He lay flat, feet against the advancing compaction plate, hands against the tailgate. His elbows and knees buckled. *Sharp things stuck into his ribs. His knees pressed against* his chest, his head against the tailgate. *This is it. I'm dead.*

Suddenly the truck stopped. The tailgate opened, and he tumbled out. The robot arm emptied another trash can, and the truck was on its way.

Ethan lay on the asphalt, panting. The panic button. He felt for it, took it out of his pocket, and turned it on. The red circle glowed in the night. He breathed a long sigh of relief.

Suddenly he heard a voice.

"What's this?"

"Dunno," said another voice. "Oversize raccoon?"

Ethan looked up. Three black teenagers were staring curiously at him. One of them bent down and examined his face.

"Wait—it's a white guy," he said.

"No way," said another, bending down as well. "Shit, he stinks worse than a skunk."

"Hey, bro," said the first one. "Do you speak? What's that in your hand?"

Ethan's heart raced. "Nothing," he said, putting the panic button hurriedly back in his pocket.

"Oh, he's got something to hide," said one of the teen-agers.

Ethan scrambled to his feet. "I'll be on my way, then," he said, stumbling.

"You OK?" said the teenager, grabbing his arm.

Ethan jerked away. *They're going to steal the panic button.* His heart raced faster.

"Suit yourself," said the teenager.

"What are you doing here?" said the third one. "Do you know where you are?"

Ethan shook his head, backing away.

"You're in the Black sector," said the teenager. "How'd you get in?"

Ethan turned and bolted, but one of the teenagers tripped him. All three laughed.

"Let's turn him in," said another.

"Maybe after he's shown us his toy."

"Get away from me," said Ethan, trying to get up.

One of the teenagers reached down. *The panic button!* thought Ethan with a flash of terror, and punched the teen-ager's arm. The teenager kicked him in the chest, and he fell back, hitting his head on the asphalt. *I'm done for!*

"Stop!" yelled a woman's voice. The teenagers froze.

"What the hell is going on?" said the woman in a heavy Jamaican accent.

"Mom!" said one of the teenagers. "What are you doing here?"

"Pipe down."

The teenager glared at her. She peered down at Ethan.

"What did they do to you?" she asked.

"They hit me," said Ethan. "They were trying to steal my phone."

"That's a lie!" yelled the teenager.

"You're in big trouble, Deion," said the woman. "You two—disappear," she said to the others.

They stood around looking mad.

"Disappear! Now!" she yelled.

They started sulkily walking away.

"You're coming home with me right now," said the woman to Deion, grabbing him by the elbow. "Come on."

The teenager started following her, cursing under his breath.

Ethan tried to get up, groaned in pain, and fell back down.

The woman stopped and turned around. "You OK, mister?" she said.

"Ah . . . not really," heaved Ethan.

"Deion, help him get up," she said.

"That's what I was trying to do," said the boy.

His mother flashed him a look of warning.

"What happened to you?" she said to Ethan.

"I, er, fell into a garbage truck."

"Are you messing with me?"

Ethan shook his head.

She gave him a look of pity. "You need a shower," she said. "And your clothes washed."

Ethan nodded hesitantly.

"Come," she said, "we live just down the street."

They started walking. A block ahead, a group of people emerged into the ghostly cone of light of a streetlamp, headed toward them.

"Guards!" said the woman. "Cross the street!"

They hurried across. Ethan stumbled on a tuft of grass growing out of a crack in the pavement. "Ouch!"

"Shhh!" said the woman.

They resumed going down the street. "Walk normally," she said.

Ethan spied the Guards out of the corner of his eye as they trundled past. They looked like hoodlums with random pieces of tactical gear thrown on.

"What was that?" he asked.

"Community Guards. You don't have them in the White sector?"

"Yeah, but they dress differently there. None of the tactical gear, just black armbands with 'CG' on them."

They kept walking and then crossed back. Finally the woman and her son stopped in front of a house that looked even more run-down than the rest.

"Here we are," she said. "After you."

7

WHAT'S A BLACK MOTHER TO DO?

Inside, the house was clean and bright. *Wow,* thought Ethan. *It looked so derelict from the outside.*

"We don't renovate the exterior," said the woman, as if reading his mind. "If you do, the Guards know you have money and come extract some."

Ethan nodded uncertainly.

"Here," she said, rummaging through a drawer and pulling out a pair of shorts and a Tshirt. "Wear these while I throw your clothes in the washer. They're Deion's. I'm Jalissa, by the way."

"I'm Ethan. Nice to meet you."

"The bathroom is down the hallway on the left," she said.

Ethan went in, closed the door and noticed a rancid smell. He looked around and jumped at the scary man in camouflage face paint looking back at him. Then he realized it was himself in the mirror. The stench was him too. He got out of his clothes and jumped in the shower with a grunt of relief.

When he came out of the bathroom, dirty clothes in hand, Jalissa was sitting at the kitchen table, typing on an old laptop. Deion was plopped down on the couch, scrolling through his phone. A strangely catchy melody filled the air.

Jalissa looked up. "Wow, you look like a regular human being now," she said. "Not like the Creature from the Black Lagoon."

Deion started laughing. Ethan felt his face grow hot.

"Here, let me take those," said Jalissa, grabbing Ethan's dirty clothes. She disappeared into the hallway, and a minute later he heard the sound of the washer running.

Ethan sat at the kitchen table and tried to place the song that was playing. He couldn't decide if he'd heard it before. Jalissa came back and started typing again.

"So what do you do for a living?" asked Ethan.

"I'm a music listener," she said.

"Huh?"

"I listen to computer-generated songs all day long."

"Wow. You get paid to do that?"

"You bet. A dollar fifty per song."

"Just to listen to them?"

"No, to hum them. Or some of them."

Ethan shook his head uncomprehendingly.

"Happinet pays me," she said. "I listen to a bunch of songs one day, and then they check which ones I'm humming the next."

"Ah."

"And then their computers generate variations of those songs and send them to other people to see which ones they hum. Do it enough times, and you get some very catchy songs. That's how they generate hits."

"Ha."

"They also send me dance music to see how my body reacts. And the sniffer tracks how I respond to all of it."

"Nice job if you can get it."

She gave him a hard look. "Except I can't stand listening to music anymore. It makes me want to throw up."

"I'm sorry."

"And I'm continuously rated on how well the songs I hummed turn out. If my rating falls too low, I can't get any more work."

"That must be stressful."

She shrugged irritably. "So how did you fall into a garbage truck?"

"I was, er, trying to retrieve something."

"Did you?"

Ethan nodded.

"Your cell phone?" asked Deion from the couch.

"Kind of."

"Kind of?" said Jalissa. "What's kind of a cell phone?"

"It's a device I'm, er, testing."

"Ah. So you're some kind of engineer."

"Yeah."

"You don't work for Happinet, do you?"

"No, no. God forbid. I work for a small company. How old is he?" Ethan asked, with a nod toward Deion.

"Eighteen."

"So who you gonna vote for, Deion?"

"PresiBot. It's super awesome."

"You don't like Raging Bull?"

"Nah. Angry old man."

"What about USA vs. FIN?"

Deion shrugged. "All the same to me."

"You like the Guards?"

"Hell no. Fuck the Guards."

"Well, if you and your friends all vote for PresiBot, maybe he'll abolish them."

"Yeah, right."

"I promise."

Deion broke into a smile. "And who are you to promise that?"

"PresiBot's maker."

Deion started laughing.

"You don't know who I am?" said Ethan.

"You're some crazy white guy."

Ethan opened his mouth to say something, but stopped. "You like AI?" he said finally.

"I love it. It's my favorite subject."

"How much do you know?"

"I built my own robot."

"No way."

"Here, look."

Deion got up, went to his room and came back with a waist-high, gray plastic, humanoid robot.

"What does it do?" Ethan asked.

"It learns by imitating me. Look."

He turned on the robot and did a series of moonwalk steps. After a few seconds the robot copied him.

"Wow. Pretty good," Ethan said.

"I'm doing a startup with two of my friends," Deion said. "The two you just met," he added with a hint of resentment.

"What will it do? Robotics is a pretty saturated market."

"Don't know yet. Maybe make them real cheap and sell them in developing countries."

"Hum. Do you have a 3-D printer?"

"I wish."

"So where did you learn robotics? In school?"

"No, I don't go to school. School sucks."

"I homeschool him," Jalissa said. "What's a Black mother to do?"

"Yeah," said Ethan. Pause. "So you know robotics too?"

"No, I enrolled him in UngallEd."

The washer beeped and Jalissa went to put Ethan's clothes in the dryer.

"So who're you gonna vote for?" Ethan asked her when she came back.

"I don't have time to vote."

"But if you vote for PresiBot—"

"Nothing will change."

"Well, if Raging Bull is elected, lots will change."

"Nah. Not for us."

"America will collapse."

"What difference will that make?"

Ethan was speechless for a moment, then thought. "If you had one request for PresiBot, what would it be?" he asked.

"You heard Deion. Get the fucking Guards off our backs." Ethan nodded.

They sat in silence for a while. When the dryer beeped Jalissa went and got Ethan's clothes. He went into the bathroom and changed back, making double sure to put the panic button back in his jeans pocket.

"Come," she said when he emerged. "I'll walk you to the checkpoint."

"Oh, thanks, but that's OK. Just tell me which way to go."

"Are you sure? If the Guards see you without Black company, you're in trouble."

"OK then. I appreciate it." They walked to the Bayshore wall along the nearly deserted streets, sweating in the still October heat.

"Why is everything so empty?" Ethan asked. "Where are the people?"

"They set aside a chunk of San Francisco for Blacks, but the Blacks never came," said Jalissa. "Cost of living too high."

"Even with the reparation payments?"

"That's barely enough for food."

"So these houses are empty? In one of the most expensive cities on Earth?"

She shrugged. "You're not allowed to sublet them to whites."

They passed a scrawny old tree, dead leaves from it drifting along the street. *That's odd,* thought Ethan. *There's no wind; why are the leaves drifting?* He tried to follow them with his eyes in the near-darkness, but they seemed to disappear into a hole in the ground. Then he got closer and saw that the hole was sucking in leaves and trash from all directions, some getting stuck in the grating that covered it, others going through.

"Careful," said Jalissa. "Don't trip on the vent."

"Vent?" Ethan asked, going around it. "For what?"

"For Happinet's data center. Intake for their cooling system."

"Wow, the data center extends this far from the Flower?"

"It didn't at first, but they kept adding capacity."

Wow, thought Ethan. *The sheer amount of compute they must have down there. It boggles the mind.*

The noise of cars speeding by on Highway 101, along the top of the wall, was getting louder. They turned right on Bayshore Blvd., crossing an abandoned gas station, and kept going. The wall was a long string of graffitis. "CANCEL AMERICA," said one. "—K YOU GUARDS," said another, partly painted over. "DELETE THE PRESIBOT," said a fresh-looking one. Finally they saw the checkpoint: a squat concrete building off to the side of Chavez where it passed under the freeway, with a boom gate blocking passage and a painted sign above it with the words "BELONGING ACCESS LOVE DIVERSITY" in black and "LIBERATION INCLUSION EQUITY SAFETY" in red.

"Which sector does that lead to?" Ethan asked.

"Brown," said Jalissa.

"You think they'll let me through?"

She shrugged. "I guess you'll find out."

They walked up to the entrance, where two Guards and a few other people milled about. Ethan stopped and turned to Jalissa.

"How can I thank you?" he said.

"By never showing up here again and getting my son in trouble."

He nodded and turned to leave, then hesitated.

"Can I hug you?" he asked.

"What you wanna hug me for?" she said, a tremor in her voice. "Go back to your nice life and forget you were ever here."

Ethan nodded again, looking down. "Goodbye, then," he said.

"Goodbye."

Ethan stood there as she disappeared into the night. Then he turned around and went into the building.

"ID, please," said the Guard behind the counter, a middle-aged woman with hard eyes and thin lips.

Ethan pulled it up on his phone and let her scan it, then waited as she ran it through the computer.

"Ethan Burnswagger?" she said.

"Yes."

"You're wanted for the crimes of reckless insensitivity and minority erasure."

"Huh? Must be a mistake."

She turned the screen toward him.

"Are you this person?"

It was a video of him at the Trouble Brewing Co. earlier that night, shot from the bartender's CCD-camera eyes.

"Yes. So?"

"You actively disparaged people of color and stated they are invisible to you."

"What? How?"

She rewound the video to the part where he said KumbAI didn't have any Black or Latinx programmers because there weren't any in Silicon Valley.

"That was an exaggeration," stammered Ethan. "I know there are some, of course."

"So you admit you lied."

"I was *joking.*"

"That's even worse."

"But the guy agreed with me."

"Yes, he's been charged as an accomplice."

"But—"

"As for you, you've been found guilty by a jury of 152,000 of your peers, spontaneously assembled on Happinet."

"Whoa! I'm sorry, I didn't mean to—"

"What you 'meant to' is immaterial. The sentence is offline exile for a year to life. Please hand over your electronic devices."

8

ONLY WE CAN SAVE THE PLANET

Dave Newald's estate nestled into the Santa Cruz mountains thirty miles south of San Francisco. The mansion and grounds were an imitation of Versailles, complete with parterre gardens, orangery, and Neptune fountain. On this night an event was in progress, or rather, trying to get started. PresiBot stood motionless on a dais, a banner behind him with "PresiBot 2040—Optimize America!" in large red letters. The Silicon Valley elite—or some of it—sat at linen-draped tables on the main lawn, talking animatedly, waiting for dinner. The whole KumbAI crew was there, scattered among the tables, hobnobbing with the founders and C-suite types. Arvind, Emma and Bozeau sat at the head table with Newald, Thomas Monk and Jack Ungall, also known as the three trillionaires.

Except Jack Ungall wasn't there.

Newald got up and paced around the dais, talking into his phone with growing irritation.

Arvind, sitting next to Monk, tried to make small talk with him.

"So, are you still on the board of KarmaCoin?" he asked.

"Oh no," said Monk, who wore the orange robes and

shaved head of a Buddhist monk. "I've sold all my shares and given up my seat. I want to focus on what's important now."

Arvind nodded. They were both silent for a moment.

"And that is?" Arvind asked.

"The passing of the seasons."

"Ah."

"Nanoseconds and teradollars—those are the two biggest obstacles to wisdom."

"Yeah. I know what you mean."

Newald hung up and returned to the table.

"OK, let's start without him," he said. "Is PresiBot ready?"

Arvind nodded.

Newald got up and tapped his wine glass with a fork for attention.

"Thank you all for being here," he said after the conversation had died down, "and for your support of PresiBot."

A dot of light appeared to the north, somewhere over the bay, and grew steadily larger.

"The million dollars each of you donated to be at this dinner will be a huge help. Together we can offset the millions of small donations that have been pouring into Raging Bull's coffers."

The whump-whup-whump of a helicopter was now audible, and growing louder.

"We will not let America be swept away by—"

The whump-whump-whump was now a deafening roar. The banner behind PresiBot started flapping vigorously, followed by the tablecloths. Name cards flew off and rolled across the lawn.

"What the—?" said Newald.

A geometry of blinking red lights and blinding white ones—UFO?—hovered above the stormy green sea of the lawn and slowly descended. Touchdown—the blades slowed to a stop, the helicopter's door opened, and Jack Ungall stepped out, arms outstretched to greet Newald, the dinner guests and everyone in the world.

Newald threw his napkin on the ground, got up, and walked out to meet him, cursing under his breath.

The helicopter's lights went out and they could finally see Ungall: a short, wiry man with long, slicked-back, jet-black hair, a widow's peak and a goatee, and an impish smile. He wore a dapper but rumpled black suit with a pocket square and a pointy-collared white shirt.

"Davey, you old sonofabitch!" he yelled. "How the heck are ya?"

"Good, and you?"

"Never better, old pal. Never better."

"Nice helicopter."

"It's not a helicopter, it's an aircar. I designed it. Did you notice how quiet it is?"

"No."

"Electric engine, ultralight battery, tiltrotor for VTOL and forward flight. And beautiful—so sleek, so—"

"Right. Anyway, let's head over to our table. We were about to get started without you."

Arvind and the rest got up to greet Ungall.

"This is Arvind Subramanian, the CTO of KumbAI," said Newald. "Arvind, this is Jack."

"Nice to meet you," said Arvind.

"Hi," said Ungall. "Where's Ethan Burnswagger?"

"Oh, he's, er, no longer with us. Max here is the new CEO."

"Delighted to meet you, Mr. Ungall," said Bozeau.

"And this is Emma Zong, KumbAI's Chief Data Officer."

Ungall looked Emma up and down. "Wow, data has never been sexier," he said. "I like your pink hair."

"Nice to meet you," said Emma, blushing.

Arvind glared at Ungall but bit his lip.

"Hi Jack," said Monk wearily.

"Thomas! Almost didn't recognize you there for a second. That your new incarnation?"

Monk gave him a stony stare.

"OK, let's resume," said Newald. "Everyone! As I was saying, with the help of all of us, PresiBot will save America from extinction. We've had our differences in the past," he said, unwittingly looking down at Ungall, "but we're united in this fight. Cheers to PresiBot!"

Everyone raised their glasses.

"And now a few words from the candidate."

Awakened by this sentence, PresiBot delivered its pre-canned speech and fell silent again. Everyone clapped politely and went back to their conversations.

A woman in an ill-fitting evening gown ambled up to the edge of the dais, probably hoping to chat with PresiBot. Arvind quickly got up and inserted himself between her and the robot.

"Hi," he said. "PresiBot is, er, doing a software update right now."

"Oh," she said. "Are you part of, um, KumbAI?"

"Yes, I'm the CTO."

"Ah, great. I'm the CEO of Cleanspeak."

Arvind looked at her blankly.

"You know, the app that makes your speech politically correct in real time? When you're on the phone?"

"Yeah, I think that rings a bell somewhere."

"Anyway, I was wondering if PresiBot would have any use for our system."

"Oh, we've got that taken care of, but thanks. Enjoy the evening."

Actually wouldn't be a bad idea to have a custom module for that, he thought, sitting back down. *Maybe I'll ping her later.*

"—and that's why I back PresiBot," Ungall was saying. "Once the president is replaced by AI, the rest of the government will follow. Think of the savings—all those incompetent government workers gone, replaced by machines. Incorruptible machines." He banged his fist on the table, making the silverware jump. "The fewer humans in government, the better."

I could be coding right now, thought Arvind.

"Besides, I know a good publicity stunt when I see one," added Ungall, looking at PresiBot.

"You really think that PresiBot will be able to govern the country?" asked Monk.

"Nah, not really," chortled Ungall. "I just want to destroy the government."

"Huh?"

"Look at it this way: if PresiBot works, great. If not, great, too. The government is long overdue for some creative destruction."

"That sounds like an argument for voting for Raging Bull."

"No, that one is just destructive destruction."

"Whatever you say, Jack."

"What about you? Why did you decide to back PresiBot? Doesn't seem like quite your cup of ginseng tea."

"Oh, it's strictly a lesser of two evils type of thing. Boy, it's hot."

"Yeah, the climate is going downhill pretty fast," said Newald.

Waiters bearing an assortment of entrees and side dishes emerged from the house and fanned out to the tables.

"I've got that problem solved," said Ungall.

"How's that?"

"You haven't heard of my new geoengineering scheme?"

"I don't think so."

"I'm going to put a shield at a Lagrange point between the Earth and the Sun."

"Better be a big one."

"Yeah, it'll take a while to assemble, but it'll be worth it."

"Too expensive."

"No, with my SE-9 rockets on a rotation from their base in the Ungall Islands, it's quite feasible."

"Forgive me for asking," said Arvind, "but what are the Ungall Islands?"

"Oh, it's the country I bought, I mean, the islands I bought, so I can build the world's only truly free country there."

"How's that going?" said Newald.

"Well, it's still in beta, but in the meantime I get to use it as the home base for my space program."

"You own an entire country?" said Emma. "No way!"

"Yep. Wanna visit?"

"I'd love to!"

"Well, we're just really busy right now," said Arvind, kicking her under the table.

"My geoengineering scheme is much better," said Newald.

"Uh-huh," said Ungall.

"Genetically engineered, ultra-fast-growing plankton. Will get us to net zero practically overnight."

Ungall started laughing.

"What?"

"That won't work."

"Why not?"

"*The fish will eat it.*"

"No, it'll oscillate, but on average—"

"On average, your geoengineering schemes are a joke. You should focus on cutting emissions, and leave the geo-engineering to me."

"You mean you don't have an emissions program? Pathetic."

"Of course I do. Scrubbers, cement, agriculture, you name it."

"Those are all low-hanging fruit. The really tough nut to crack is air travel."

"I'm on that as well."

"Your aircopter over there?"

"Aircar. No, that helps, but it's just for regional travel. I'm talking about the World Wide Subway."

"Ah, the one that's always only a few years away? The most over-budget project in history?"

"New York to Shanghai in thirty minutes, and no emissions."

"But your trains keep blowing up."

"Well, when you're going twenty thousand miles per hour, every little molecule of air turns into a killer missile. And when you have to do it halfway around the Earth, it's like being bombarded by—"

"Doesn't sound promising."

"We just need better pumps. Pumps are what's holding us up. Anyway, how's your moon base?"

"The repairs are almost complete. We should resume flights within a year. I'll still beat you to Jupiter."

"But I'll beat you to Saturn."

"Wanna bet?"

Ungall hesitated for a moment.

"Whatever," he said. "What are you doing about emissions?"

"Cows that don't burp. Does away with a lot of methane."

"Nah, that's weak," said Ungall. "But that's OK. I have a geoengineering scheme for you. You know what you should do?"

"No, tell me."

"Extend the Flower up. Make it ten times taller, at least. Then inject sulfates at the bottom. The Flower spews them out at the top, they spread, and voilà—a nice cheap way to reflect a lot of solar radiation away."

"Ha ha."

"And as a bonus, that white elephant of a building would finally have a reason to exist."

"That one," said Newald, putting down his fork, "is a little too much."

"Well, I'm glad we're all trying different things," said Monk quickly, "because one of them better work. If we wait around for governments to do something, we're doomed. Only we can save the planet."

Newald and Ungall nodded at the same time.

They ate in silence for a while.

"Isn't it amazing how random life is?" Monk said. "Here we are, but one flap of the butterfly's wings and we could have been hobos sleeping under the stars."

"Speak for yourself, buddy," Ungall said. "I was destined to succeed."

"How do you see a butterfly changing your fate?" Arvind asked Monk.

"Well, you know. It starts a storm, I stay at home that day instead of going to work, and I'm never in the meeting that gave me the idea for KarmaCoin."

"That wouldn't make you a hobo, just not rich."

"Don't be so literal-minded, grasshopper."

"Butterflies, grasshoppers . . . me, I'm more into the birds and the bees," said Ungall, looking at Emma. Emma looked away.

"Serendipity is a big part of life," said Newald. "We try to foster that with Happinet."

"As long as those serendipitous events put more money in your pocket," said Ungall.

"No, we just try to make people happy."

"Oh yes, making them want things they can't afford really does that."

"Happiness is not a state, it's a striving. Our advertisers give people things to strive for."

"How convenient. Me, I prefer to just give people things," Ungall said, counting them off on his fingers. "Zero

Click gives them predictive delivery. Ride'n'Roll gives them a ride anywhere, anytime. Answers4All answers all their questions. UngallEd gives them an education. And Arrow-Gant Space Industries will—"

"Spare us."

They heard a ping, and Ungall looked at his phone.

"Check this out," he said to Newald, "I just passed you again as the world's richest man."

"How can that be? The markets are closed."

"After-hours trading."

"That doesn't count."

"Just wait for tomorrow morning, then."

"Won't last. Wait a week."

"Sure, Dave. How much more overvalued can Happinet get? Won't be long before it comes crashing back down to Earth."

"No, we're just getting started. Unlike you, who are yesterday's news."

"Oh yeah? Where are you going to find more users? On Mars, once you're done colonizing it? Or have the markets already priced that in?"

"You're just jealous because you didn't invent the neurosniffer."

"Yeah, why didn't I invent a fake emotion detector, like you? And then I could con advertisers into thinking I can read users' minds, like you. And build a whole empire on fraud and crap code, like you."

"Are you saying the sniffer is fake? I'll sue your ass for defamation."

"You know very well what I'm saying," said Ungall with a

shrug. "Your sniffer's accuracy is barely better than chance. Just enough signal that you're not outright lying when you say it predicts emotions, but not nearly good enough to do anything useful. Oops, should I not have said that in front of our impressionable young guests?"

"Ha ha. Really. So how come our clickthrough rate is higher than anyone's? Is that fraud too?"

"No, it's all those thousands of data monkeys you have desperately mining every last shred of data you can get your greedy hands on. But that's not nearly as sexy, of course."

"Aha! So you admit it works!"

"Actually, not even. Your clickthrough rate is pathetic. It's better than the rest just because you have way more data."

"Talk is cheap! Prove it!"

"Easy. How much do you make per user per year? Less than a thousand bucks, even though the average user makes over a hundred thousand. Less than one percent—that's the extent of Happinet's 'mind control'! Ooh, I'm so scared! Happinet can play my brain like a clarinet! The only reason you're a multi-trillion dollar company is that you have so many users—and you've scammed the market into believing your bullshit!"

Newald got up and shoved his finger in Ungall's face. "Shut the fuck up or I'll kick your ass!"

"Go ahead! Go right ahead, fucker!" yelled Ungall, grabbing a lobster and flinging it at Newald.

Newald jumped on the table to lunge at Ungall, but the table swung and hit him in the face, sending food flying everywhere. Newald landed hard on his back, but scrambled to his feet and ran around, fists swinging. Ungall ducked and landed one squarely on Newald's jaw. Newald flung himself at him, and they rolled around on the lawn, punching, biting, grappling with each other. Hector, Newald's security chief, came running, dove into the melee, and finally managed to separate them.

"Boss! Boss! What are you doing?"

"Kick the fucker out! Throw him back in his fucking helicopter and kick him out! Go! Go!"

"Yes, boss. Right away, boss!"

Hector dragged and frog-marched Ungall to his aircar.

"Let me go!" yelled Ungall, kicking him. "Let go of my collar! You don't have the right! Let me go!"

Ungall's bodyguard came running toward them.

"Hey!" he said. "What the hell are you doing? Stop that!"

"Here!" said Hector, pushing Ungall toward him. "Take him!"

"You're a fucking loser, Dave!" yelled Ungall as he got into his aircar. "Crappinet sucks! And you'll never be a quadrillionaire!"

Moments later the aircar rose into the night sky and was gone. Newald went into the house, wiping clumps of grass and Beluga caviar off his face and T-shirt.

There was a moment of stunned silence, then everyone looked away and started chattering again.

"Wow, that was . . . intense," said Arvind.

"Oh, they do this every time they meet," said Monk.

On their way back, as their Happinet limo wound its way around the 280 freeway's potholes and stopped at checkpoints to pay transit fees to the Guards, Arvind was pensive. *Why am I involved with these people? They make*

Raging Bull look like a saint. How did I get into this? And how do I get out?

"What's wrong?" said Emma.

"Sometimes I miss being a grad student," said Arvind.

"Why? That was fun. Even the fight."

"Really? I don't think our two biggest backers getting into a fistfight at a fundraising dinner is good for the campaign. And I think—"

"You think too much."

"I don't know. Let me think about it."

"Live a little, for a change."

"I don't want to deal with this bullshit. I want to do research."

"Me, I wanna be rich like them."

"Is that all you can think of? Money?"

"Easy for you to say, mister. I grew up in a tenement."

"All this 'I'm richer than you' crap means nothing to me."

"You're boring."

"Sometimes I don't know if I really want PresiBot to win."

9

ETHAN'S RUN

Ethan looked at the Guard, heart racing.

"I'm sorry, I can't do that," he said finally.

"Tyler!" shouted the Guard. "Confiscate his electronics!"

"Sure," said Tyler. "Just as soon as I'm done feeding the baby."

"Now!"

Ethan glanced quickly around. There seemed to be only two other Guards in the room, and they were both at their desks.

He spun around and dashed for the door.

"Aha!" said the Guard, pushing a button. The door bolted shut and an alarm went off, strobing the room with a lurid red light and piercing Ethan's ears with its whine.

Ethan turned, dodged the Guard, and ran across the room to the corridor at the back. There was a door at the end of the corridor—locked. He turned around. Four Guards and a screaming baby were barreling toward him down the corridor. He tried a door on his right—open. It was a bathroom. He locked the door and jumped on the toilet to get to the tiny window above it. He unlatched the window and pushed it, but it didn't budge. The Guards were banging on the door. "Go around!" yelled one. Finally the window flew open, and Ethan clambered through it, head first, then torso, then legs— His shoelace caught on the latch and left him dangling upside down, his face a foot from the ground. Shouts in the dark, a flashlight rapidly approaching. Ethan shoved his foot free and tumbled onto the ground, hurting his wrist, crying out. He struggled onto his feet and tried to get his bearings. The flashlight was upon him, so he just ran in the opposite direction.

He was on the street, running down Chavez. Roused by the alarm, people were coming out of their houses, pointing at him. Someone was running close behind him.

"Hey! Hey!" said the man.

Ethan ran faster, but the man kept up.

"Aren't you the KumbAI guy? Ethan Burnswagger?" yelled the man.

"What do you want?" said Ethan without looking back.

"I saw you at the checkpoint. I just want to interview you."

"What?"

"I'm from the *New York Times*."

"What's the *New York Times*?"

"A newspaper."

"Oh wow, they still make those?"

They were at the intersection with Van Ness. Ethan swerved right, and the reporter slammed into a lamppost. Up ahead, Ethan saw a truck speeding away. With a last rush of energy, he caught up with it and jumped onto the step bumper. Clinging to the roll-up door's handle, he tried to turn it. Miracle! It opened. Ethan pushed the door up, slid inside and crumpled onto the floor.

"Whew!" he said out loud.

"Hey!" said a sleepy voice. "What's going on?"

Ethan jumped to his feet and almost fell out of the truck. A small light came on, and he could make out a disheveled old man, leaning on his elbow, blinking awake.

"Er . . . I'm sorry—really sorry," said Ethan. "Just hitching a quick ride, if that's OK."

"No, not OK. Get the hell out of my truck."

"I will, I will, as soon as it stops."

The man fumbled around and sat up with a gun in his hand. "Out. Now!"

"All right, all right." Ethan glanced dubiously out of the semi-open door. "You know, if I hurt myself, you're liable. Even if I'm trespassing."

The man considered this.

"Screw it," he said finally. "Stay right where you are, then. And close that damn door."

"Can I sit?"

"OK. Don't try anything funny, or I'll shoot."

Ethan carefully closed the door and sat down. *He's gonna kick me out at the first red light,* he thought. *No. Keep him talking.*

"So you're the owner of this truck?" he said.

"No, I'm the driver."

"But you're, er, not driving."

"Of course not. The truck does that. I'm just the backup."

"Shouldn't you be in the cab?"

"Hah, why bother? If it's gonna crash, it's gonna crash."

"Why are you here, then?"

"In case anything goes wrong, smartass."

"What do you mean?"

"Say the truck runs someone over. It's my fault for not intervening."

"Aha."

"This way the self-driving system is never at fault."

"But now they have to pay you. Defeats the point, no?"

"Oh, they pay me far less than if I was actually driving the rig. And it's worth it. If the AI gets blamed, they'd have to recall it, ground the fleet, what have you. If I get blamed— well, it's just me," he said, with an edge of bitterness.

"How long have you been doing this?"

"Since they— since—"

Suddenly the man burst into tears. "It's not right!" he sobbed. "It's not fucking right! This *used* to be my truck!"

"I know how you feel," Ethan said.

"What are *you* doing here, anyway?" growled the man, shoving the gun in Ethan's face.

"Wait, wait," said Ethan. "I don't know where to begin."

"I'm listening."

"The Guards are trying to confiscate my . . . er . . . phone."

"Why?"

"Something I said."

"Fucking Guards. Can't fucking stand them."

"Me neither," said Ethan cautiously.

"All they do is make normal people's life hell."

"Right, right."

"They harass me every day of the week, and all the while let criminals run free. Hell, criminals run this country."

"Couldn't agree more."

"Pretty soon there'll be no country."

"Yeah, we have to stop that Raging Bull guy."

"Goddamn redskin. Thinks he owns the place. Did you see the AK-47? How the fuck did they allow that in a presidential debate?"

"He demanded it."

"What?"

"He said PresiBot is a prop, so he's entitled to one as well. Besides, Wolf News liked it—good for the ratings."

"You're kidding."

"It has no bullets, of course."

"Yeah right. How do you know?"

"Oh, I, er, read it somewhere. Seriously, it's public knowledge."

"Not that that fucking robot is much better."

"Well, at least it's—"

"Fucking tool of the fat cats. And fucking dumb, too. Better at least have a backup driver."

"Heuh . . . erm . . . that's not a bad idea."

"Elect that tin can, and anyone who still has a job can kiss it goodbye."

"Well, not necessarily."

"Huh?"

"There's much harder jobs than president, actually. Like plumber, for example. Presidents can delegate everything. A plumber needs real—"

The trucker burst out laughing. "You're a funny guy," he said.

"PresiBot's not that bad, you know," insisted Ethan. "It's just trying to maximize the expected utility of all Americans."

"Come again?"

"You know, make everyone happy."

"Ha ha. That's what they all say."

"But between the two, you'll vote for PresiBot, right?"

"I guess," said the trucker grudgingly. "Save the ol' US of A, and all that. We made this country. Can't let it fall back into the hands of the sav—"

Suddenly the truck screeched to a halt, sending them tumbling.

"What the fuck?!" yelled the trucker, jumping up.

"Get out of the truck," said a voice through a bullhorn. "Hands in the air."

"Shit," said the trucker. "Roadblock. We're screwed."

He opened the tailgate and stepped out gingerly, hands high up.

"All right, all right," he said. "No need to—ow!"

Ethan's thoughts raced. Hide the panic button in the truck? He'd never see it again. Run away through the streets? They seemed to be surrounded. With a sinking feeling, he realized there was only one option left. He took a deep breath. Jumping out of the truck, he ducked, slid around the side, clambered into the cab, hit the override button and gunned the engine as the mob converged on him. The truck crashed through the barrier and roared down the street.

Ethan glanced at the rearview mirror, trying to see how far behind him the mob was.

"Whoa!"

Another mob had just emerged from a side street ahead, heading toward him. He swerved violently to avoid them. The truck flipped and slid to a halt, and he banged his head on the windshield and fell onto the driver-side window. Climbing to the passenger side, he clambered out of the cab and ran across the street and several blocks down a side street. He turned randomly into another street, then another. Without stopping, he glanced over his shoulder to see if the mob was still chasing him, and—Ouch! He tripped on something and fell flat on his face. *What the—?* A steel grating—he was face down on it, looking through it, at what seemed like a concrete ramp descending into darkness. A draft blew past his cheeks and into the opening. *Oh, it's another one of those vents.* Clambering to his knees, he could see why he had tripped: the grating wasn't properly closed, and one end protruded above the pavement. The roar of the mob was getting closer. Suddenly he had an idea. He pulled at the grating—it was heavy, but he could just about lift it—and he slid his body into the vent—hold, hold—an incongruous vision of Newald bench pressing flitted through his mind—and once he was all in he let go of the grating, which thumped back into place an inch from his nose. A succession of feet pounded on the grating—a white rubber sole landed right above is face and he stifled a cry—and—aargh! He was sliding down the vent—nothing to hold on to—his hands clutching in vain—falling faster—until he came to a stop on a level surface.

Lifting his head, he looked around. In front of him to each side, a row of servers stretched away to infinity, lights blinking, fans purring. Pale blue light shone down from above, a traffic jam of cables running along the ceiling. *I'm dead,* he thought for a moment. *This is the afterlife—I've awoken from the simulation.* Then the pain in the back of his skull brought him back to reality. *I need to get out of here.* He got back on his feet, put a foot on the ramp—

A sound in his ear. Faint, distant. Music? He turned around and tried to place it. It seemed to be coming from the right. He started walking in that direction, tentatively at first, then faster. On one side, a concrete wall with no end in sight—he seemed to be on the edge of the data center. On the other, more and more rows of servers. The music was louder now—someone singing. He recognized the melody: "Under the Boardwalk". Several more rows of servers and he could make out the words:

Under the Flo-o-wer
Down by the servers, yeah
On a blanket tryin'a sleep some
Is where I'll be

A faint smell now—cooking? Tortillas? The song continued:

Under the Flower
Out of the street
Under the Flower
Find me somethin' to eat
Under the Flower
People working above
Under the Flower
We're just tryin'a survive
Under the Flower, Flower

This must be the row it's coming from, Ethan thought. He started to peek around the corner, but suddenly something sharp poked into his ribs from behind. "Don't move," said a voice.

"I'm not moving," said Ethan. *Christ,* he thought. *What now?*

"Hands on your head." Ethan obeyed, palms clammy. "Now walk." Ethan started forward. "No, not that way. Left, between the servers."

Ethan walked a few dozen yards down the server corridor, knife digging between his ribs. The singing was now loud and clear, and finally it ended in a burst of clapping. Up ahead, he could see a group of people squatting on the ground, talking and laughing, but there was something odd about them. Their bodies seemed to shimmer in and out of existence in the dim light, like a wavy mirage of distorted server racks. When he got closer he could see they wore some sort of reflective clothing. Suddenly they stopped talking and looked at him, and he could see the "R"s on their foreheads.

"Hey guys," said the voice behind him. "Look what I found spying on us."

"No way, José," said one of the squatters, a muscular man with long black hair.

"Yes, way," said José. "He was at the end of our row, peeking around a network cabinet."

The other squatter, a bull-necked man with a shaved head and tank top, looked at him doubtfully.

"I swear, Leon."

"I wasn't spying on anyone," Ethan said.

"What were you doing, then?" Leon said. "Do you live here?"

"Live here?" Ethan said. "What are you talking about?"

"Are you a Guard?"

"Do I look like a Guard?"

"Anyone can look like a Guard."

"Nah, he's too young," said another squatter.

"Shut up, Mikey."

Suddenly a burning smell, and smoke coming from the open door of a server cabinet.

"Mikey, you idiot," said Leon. "Did you burn the tortillas?"

"No," said Mikey, hurriedly collecting the sizzling tortillas from the tops of the servers, "but this rack does seem hotter than usual."

Mikey passed the tortillas around, and they started to eat.

"So you're not robots," Ethan said.

The squatters burst into laughter.

"No," said Leon, "but painting the 'R's on our foreheads confuses the surveillance system. Between that and the tin foil, we can pretty much do anything we want without getting caught."

"Seriously? You think you can fool the system that easily?"

"What would you know, genius?"

"I work on state-of-the-art—"

"You think the surveillance tech down here is state-of-the-art?"

Ethan bit his lip, then said, "But the maintenance crews will get you."

"They're all robots, dummy. Also not state-of-the-art.

Besides, we know how to hide from them."

"On that subject, where is *your* tin foil, bozo?" said José, poking him with the knife. "You're going to get us all caught, and then where will we live? Back on the street?"

"Sorry, I just—"

"Mikey, wrap this guy in tin foil before I whack him," said Leon. "And paint an R on his forehead while you're at it."

Mikey went off to get the tin foil and paint. Ethan didn't feel the knife on his back any more, but José was still behind him.

"Keep very, very still until you're wrapped," said Leon.

Ethan started to nod but then caught himself.

"Now," said Leon. "How did you get in here?"

"I fell into a vent," said Ethan.

"Really. How did that happen?"

"The grating was sticking up."

Leon looked past Ethan at José. "José? Did you not lock the vent on your way down?"

"I— I—" stammered José.

"What a fucking idiot," said Leon, getting up and drawing a machete from his back. "I've had it with you."

"No! Wait! We need to deal with this guy first!"

Leon paused, twirling the machete. "OK, first things first." He squatted down again, but continued playing with the machete. "So, mister, what shall we do with you?"

"Just let me go."

"How do we know you won't rat on us?"

"I won't. I swear."

"Easy to say. I think we'll just have to keep you down here."

"Bad idea. I'll wind up giving you away."

"Maybe we should just bump you off, then."

"You wouldn't do that, would you? You're such nice people."

"You gotta do what you gotta do."

"Squatting is one thing. Premeditated murder is another."

"Not murder, just an accident. You bit one of the cables and swallowed too much data."

The others laughed. "Information overdose," said one.

"Listen," said Ethan, "it's very important that I get out of here. I have some urgent things to do."

"I remember when my life used to be like that. But now I'm free."

"Just tie him up," said another squatter.

"And let him enjoy his newfound freedom," said José, and the others started laughing.

Mikey returned with the tin foil and paint, and proceeded to wrap Ethan and paint an "R" on his forehead.

"Anyone have some rope?" asked Leon.

The others shook their heads.

"Come on, someone must have some rope."

"Here, use this Ethernet cable."

Leon tied Ethan's hands tight behind his back.

"Come on guys, there's no need for this," said Ethan.

"I need another one for his legs," said Leon. "Anyone have another spare cable?"

No one volunteered any.

"Why don't you use the same cable to tie him to a server rack?" said José. "Then he can't get away."

"Good idea," said Leon, kicking Ethan's legs out from under him and then dragging him on the floor until he had his back to a server rack. He tied one end of the cable to a rail and pulled tight. "Alrighty," he said. "Let's finish eating."

They continued munching on their tortillas.

"So you just have your tortillas . . . plain?" asked Ethan.

"You think we're rich, or something?" Leon said.

"If only we could eat electricity, we'd be all set," said another squatter, a gaunt, youngish-looking woman. "Right, Gibbon?" she said to the ponytailed young man squatting next to her with his arm around her, one eye covered by a cheap plastic display.

"Huh?" he said, removing one of his earbuds.

"Too bad we can't eat electricity."

"I'd settle for ramen, like in my grad student days," he said.

"You used to be a grad student?" said Ethan, astonished.

"Yeah. Psychology."

"And?"

"I wrote a paper on VDD."

"What's that?"

"Victimhood delusion disorder. People who empathize so much with a minority they hallucinate they're members of it."

"That's a real thing? They're not just faking it to get ahead?"

"Oh, it's very real. In fact, there's an epidemic of it."

"You're kidding."

"I wish. Problem is, these days there are many people in positions of power with a serious case of VDD, and the whole concept is threatening to them."

"You must be a real fan of Raging Bull."

"Don't get me started."

"So what happened?"

"When I tried to publish the paper, all hell broke loose. I was kicked out of Berkeley and sentenced offline by the Guards. And then I was on the black list—I couldn't rent an apartment, get a job, or even a train ticket. I was sleeping rough and . . . That was when I met Alice, who brought me down here. Thanks, Alice."

"I love you, honey," she said. "Maybe we can get some ramen on our next expedition to the surface."

"I don't like going to the surface anymore," Gibbon said. "It's too risky. Besides, it's nice and cool down here."

"Unless you catch a cold from the draft," said a raspy female voice behind them.

"Mila back there got sentenced offline for attempting to cross into the Black sector without proper paperwork," said Leon.

"I did have it, but there was a typo," said Mila.

"And Alice got sentenced for . . . what was it? Posting disinformation on Happinet?" said Gibbon.

Alice shrugged. "Who cares?

"Me, I still don't know what I got exiled for," said José.

"Probably something you should have said, but didn't," said Alice.

"Or just someone who didn't like you," said Gibbon.

"So this is where all the offline exiles go when they disappear," said Ethan in wonderment.

"We're not all exiles," said Leon. "Some of us just lost our postage stamps."

"Beg pardon?"

"You don't know the joke?"

"What joke?"

"What do you call a ten million-dollar postage stamp?" Ethan shook his head.

"An apartment in San Francisco," said Leon, and a few of the squatters chuckled.

"Ah."

"I used to rent a basement down in Ingleside, but then I lost my job and the landlord kicked me out."

"So you're not from the Brown sector?"

"We're from every sector. There're no walls down here."

"Wow. How many of you are there?"

"Thousands, probably. Not sure. We don't go in other people's territory."

"But *our* territory keeps shrinking," complained Mila. "I used to go rollerblading everywhere. Now . . . yuck."

"Happinet better expand their data center again soon, or we're in trouble," said Gibbon.

"It's all those people ratting on each other just to get ahead," said Leon.

"Pretty soon there won't be anyone left above ground," said Alice.

"Except Dave Newald and his pals," said Leon.

"His turn will come," said Mila.

"Ha," said Leon.

"Personally, I have nothing against Newald," said Alice. "Happinet provides us with free housing, and with Internet service included."

The others chuckled.

"Lightning fast, too," said José. "Just plug directly into a snitch, I mean, switch."

"We're just lucky Newald got into a pissing contest with Jack Ungall about who had the fastest response times," said Gibbon, "or this data center wouldn't even be here."

"I've heard some of the server farms up in Oregon are pretty swank," said Mikey.

"Well, move your ass up there, then," said Leon. "What are you waiting for?"

"I like the people here," protested Mikey. "Except you."

Leon tried to swat him, but he'd already jumped away. The others laughed.

"You're just jealous I have a job," said Mikey from a safe distance.

"You call your gig entering captchas for a Russian gang a job?" said Mila.

"It pays for tortillas."

"But how do the rest of you make money?" Ethan asked.

"I could tell you, but then I'd have to kill you," Leon said, running his finger along the blade of his machete.

After a while the squatters started falling asleep one by one.

Ethan tried very carefully to pry his hands loose from the rack, but no luck. He tried again—nope. Dammit! He clenched his fists, and the right one brushed against the edge of the rail. He felt it with his fingers—surprisingly sharp. He pushed the Ethernet cable against the edge and patiently started to drag it up and down. Getting through the plastic sheath was the easy part. There—he could feel the copper mesh of the shielding rubbing against the steel of the rail's edge. One by one the thin copper wires snapped. Yes! On to the insulation—harder plastic, but still plastic. But the core—this wasn't going to work against the thick core wire. In desperation, he kept rubbing. The rail's edge was hot against his wrists. He pulled—nope. He continued dragging the wire up and down against the rail. Pull again—still nope. His wrists hurt. He pulled again, harder—yes! The wire snapped, and he was free from the rack. But his hands were still tied behind his back.

A squatter stirred, disturbed by the noise, and Ethan froze. All was silent again, save for the squatters' snoring.

Now to get up. Leaning against the servers, he edged his back up little by little until he was squatting and then stood up. He stood still for a moment, listening for any signs of life from the squatters. Nothing. He started tiptoeing away down the server corridor, very slowly and with legs apart to keep the tin foil from creaking, then a little faster. He turned the corner and—squeak, went his sneaker on the linoleum, echoing across the data center like the cry of a night bird in the jungle.

"Who's there?" It was Leon's voice. "Guys! Wake up! The prowler's gone!"

Ethan bolted down the corridor, looking desperately for the vent. There! Swiveling left, he charged up the steep slope, feet sliding on the concrete, hands still tied behind his back. Lowering his head, he slammed into the grating with his back and shoulders. The grating lifted a fraction of an inch—and came down again, Ethan's soles slipping off the ground, his face coming down on it. He could hear the squatters approaching rapidly, Leon's voice yelling "Quick!

He's in the vent!" Turning onto his back, he pushed up against the grating with his feet—it lifted!—then up and forward—yes!—the grating slid forward a foot, and Ethan pushed his torso up through the crack, then—someone grabbed his foot and pulled, dragging him back down. Noo! Ethan clutched the grating for his life. His sneaker came off, a bang, a curse down below. He dragged himself back up through the crack, torso, legs, then rolled onto the sidewalk and clambered uncertainly onto his feet.

Limping, shoeless in one foot, hands tied behind his back, he ran back toward Van Ness and across it, a car honking, someone yelling "Look! Another robot's gone haywire! Call the Guards!" He looked back—the squatters were hot on his heels, at least half a dozen of them, Leon to the front, pointing. He kept running, but now the tin foil was unspooling around his legs, dragging on the pavement, tripping him up. He looked down, and that moment his foot caught in the foil and he slammed onto the ground. Dazed and in pain, he rolled around—and howled as Leon's kick ripped into his side.

"Fucker," said Leon. The others caught up and surrounded Ethan. "OK, guys, let's carry him back," said Leon. "José, take the feet. Mikey—"

But now a pickup truck screeched to a halt next to them, and one, two, three, four Guards jumped down from the back.

"Guards! Run!" yelled Gibbon.

Leon punched the nearest Guard, sending him reeling. Another Guard struck him on the side with a baseball bat, hard, and he momentarily lost balance, but he steadied himself and lunged at the Guard, who dodged.

"Leon!" yelled Alice, running. "Don't be an idiot!"

Leon hesitated for a moment, then, with a growl, rammed into the Guard blocking his way and started running, catching up with the others. As the squatters ran back toward Van Ness, chased by the Guards, Ethan looked around and—

"Oh no, buddy, you're not going anywhere," said another Guard, looming over him, his boot coming down on Ethan's chest and staying there.

10

THE LAST POLICE OFFICER IN SAN FRANCISCO

A mob had gathered around Ethan, armed with sticks, base-ball bats and metal bars.

"Is that the berserk robot?" asked a tall man in a black T-shirt, bat in hand.

"Nope," said the Guard, tapping Ethan's chest with his boot. "Flesh and blood. Don't know why he has the 'R', though."

The man leaned down to look at Ethan's face. "Isn't this the guy we were chasing earlier tonight?"

"Oh yeah," said the Guard. "Look, people, we caught the Braunschweiger guy," he announced.

"It's our lucky day," said a voice in the crowd.

"Now for the fun part," said the man in the black T-shirt.

The Guard lifted his foot off Ethan's chest. "Get up, coward," he said.

"I can't," said Ethan weakly. "My hands are tied."

The Guard crouched down and rolled Ethan around. Pulling a knife from a sheath at his side, he cut the loops of Ethernet cable around Ethan's wrists. "Now get up."

Ethan tried to sit up, but the piercing pain in his side

from Leon's kick was too great. He closed his eyes, waited a moment, then tried again. This time he managed to prop himself up on his elbows.

Without warning, the man swung the bat, but Ethan rolled away and the bat hit the ground. Ethan slid back, and his head bumped against a wall. He propped himself against it and managed to drag himself up. The man swung again, and this time it hit him squarely in the ribs, knocking the wind out of him and sending him stumbling back to the ground.

"Take that, bigot," said the man.

"Oppressor! Colonist pig!" yelled the mob, closing in on him.

Ethan stumbled back onto his feet, and quickly scanned the crowd, looking for an opening, anything. No luck.

But behind them—coming over the hill, like the cavalry riding to the rescue—

A police car.

The car stopped halfway down the hill, lights flashing.

"Disperse!" came a voice from the police car's loudspeaker.

The crowd turned around, but didn't move.

"What the—?" said the Guard.

"Disperse! Now!"

Still the crowd didn't move.

A police officer got out of the car and fired two shots into the air.

"I'm outta here," said the Guard, jumping in the pickup and speeding away.

The crowd started to edge back, and some of them ran off to the left and right.

The cop fired another shot, and lowered the gun to point at the remaining toughs.

"Shit," said the man with the bat, backing off.

"Keep going," said the cop. He swung the gun slowly from left to right and back as the last of the mob dispersed. But they hung around on the sidewalks, watching.

"You!" said the cop, pointing the gun at Ethan. "Come over here!"

Ethan walked unsteadily toward him. The cop moved aside and motioned him with the gun toward the car. Ethan stepped forward, and felt the gun against his back.

"Am I under arrest?" he said.

"No."

"Oh."

"I'm not arresting you, I'm rescuing you. Keep walking."

The mob edged closer.

"When I say 'now', run to the car and jump in," said the cop.

Ethan nodded.

"Now!"

They dashed to the car, got in and slammed the doors as the crowd surged. The cop gunned the engine and the car accelerated uphill in reverse with an ear-piercing whine. At the top of the hill the cop turned the car around and sped off toward the lights of downtown, the Flower's petals hovering above them like a mothership minding its children.

They drove in silence for a while.

"Thanks for getting me out of that jam," said Ethan.

"No worries. I'm Officer Lee, by the way."

Ethan nodded. "I'm—"

"I know who you are. Your little stunt is all over Happineighbor. How do you think that flash mob chasing you gathered?"

"Right. Should have thought of that."

"Every last sonofabitch looking for some virtuous fun on a Friday night."

"No kidding."

"But I thought you'd gotten away."

"So did I."

"What was that about a robot on the lam? And what's all that tin foil, and the 'R' on your forehead?"

"Long story," said Ethan, wondering if he should tell him about the squatters.

"You're not with the Happinet squatters, are you?"

"You know about them?"

"As you can see."

"So why don't you do something about it?"

"They have nowhere else to live."

They were silent again for a while.

"You're a cop?" said Ethan. "I thought the SFPD had been abolished."

"It was, but the police union contract didn't allow them to fire us, so they had to keep paying us."

"So how many of you are left?"

"Just me, at this point."

"Why don't you retire?"

"This pays more, and it's no more work."

"But here you are, driving around in your patrol car and rescuing people."

"That's just a hobby."

They were at the intersection of Sutter and Grant, near the Dragon Gate checkpoint into the Yellow Sector.

"I grew up there," said the cop, pointing toward the gate and the Great Wall of Chinatown.

"You're Chinese?"

"On my father's side. Mother was half Cuban and half Irish."

"Wow. I don't think that could happen today."

"Probably not."

"It's so sad that American cities are now broken up into *sectors* like this."

Officer Lee nodded. "I remember when the Guards walled off Bayview-Hunters Point to protect the black community from white intruders. What were they thinking? But before you knew it, everyone was busy walling off their territory. Only made things worse."

"Worked out well for the Guards."

"And nobody else."

They stopped at a red light, engine purring. Two late-night revelers crossed the street, laughing and stumbling.

"So where would you like me to drop you off?" said the cop.

"Er . . . home, I guess," said Ethan. "It's on Harrison, between Beale and Fremont."

The cop nodded. The light turned green, and he resumed driving.

"By the way," he said after a while, "you should be aware that you don't have to hand over your electronics when a Guard asks you to. You're entitled to a hearing."

"On Happinet? Yeah right."

"In a court of law."

"Imagine that."

"Now that truck you just overturned, that's going to be a suspended license, at least."

Ethan hung his head.

"And if the owner of the truck presses charges . . . but I don't think they will."

"Pray to God."

"What I don't understand is why you didn't just let them have your phone. Then you buy a new one, they make a few bucks selling the old one, and life goes on."

"It wasn't about the phone."

The cop glanced over at him. "What then?"

Ethan hesitated for a moment, then took the panic button out of his jeans pocket and showed it to the cop. "This."

"What's that?"

"PresiBot's panic button."

The cop looked nonplussed.

"It allows me to take control of PresiBot in case of emergency."

"What kind of emergency?"

"You know, PresiBot is a very complex AI. It can go haywire in all sorts of ways we can't predict."

"Our next president—potentially—can go haywire?"

"No more than a human," said Ethan defensively. "Just in different ways."

"Still."

"It's done OK so far. It'll probably be fine. Just a precaution."

"Or it could decide to end humanity."

Ethan sighed. "That's not going to happen."

"How do you know?"

"It's incompatible with its objective function. Trust me. What we're really worried about is it screwing up, not hatching some plan to blow up the world."

"That doesn't sound very reassuring."

"Well, with the panic button, if push comes to shove I can take over. I can become PresiBot, for all intents and purposes."

The cop was silent. He seemed to be processing this information.

"I still don't understand, though," he said finally. "Can't you just disable it, this . . . panic button?"

"Not really."

"Why?"

"It needs to be completely hack-proof. We did a pretty thorough job."

"Like, it recognizes your thumb?"

"Soon," said Ethan exasperatedly. "We haven't implemented that feature yet."

"Wait—that thing can be operated by *anyone* who gets a hold of it?"

"At this point, yes. But PresiBot is not president yet, and—"

"What were you thinking?"

"We haven't had a whole lot of time to think in the last few months, to be honest."

The cop looked horrified.

"Now you see why I didn't want it falling into the hands of the Guards," said Ethan.

"No kidding."

They were silent again for a while.

"I think I'm going to have nightmares about this," said Ethan. "I keep seeing this image of me dead on the street and the Guards and the squatters fighting over the panic button."

Officer Lee chuckled.

"You think that's funny?"

"No, I think it's democracy."

"Huh?"

"Everyone fighting over PresiBot."

"Ha ha."

"Too bad they can't each have their own panic button. Hey, I'd like one too. Make myself heard."

Ethan looked at him.

"You know, that's actually an interesting idea," he said.

"To let chaos rule?"

"No, no. Let me think."

And then it came to him.

"That's it! That's it! I know what we need to do! Yesss!"

"Huh?"

"On second thoughts, don't take me home."

"We're out of beer," said Emma, refrigerator door open. "And Diet Coke."

"Odd," said Arvind from the sofa bed a few inches away. "That shouldn't happen."

The TV was showing an old movie from the 2020s.

Arvind flipped to the news.

Emma continued to rummage through the refrigerator.

"Come to bed," said Arvind.

"There, I found one." She lay down next to him and took a swig of the beer. "I'll share it with you."

Arvind put his hand on her stomach. After a while he slid it up to her breast.

"Not yet," she said.

Arvind's hand beat a tactical retreat back down to her stomach.

"I wish we had a bigger place," said Emma.

"So do I," said Arvind.

"Do you think what Ungall said about the sniffer is true?"

"Probably."

"How do you know?"

"Like he said, if it really worked, Happinet would make way more money."

"But if he's right, that's bad news for us."

"Why?"

"Because it means Happinet can't save us."

"Well, there's still a lot we can do with all the signals they have."

"Like what?"

"Just throw them all in the optimizer."

Emma winced. "Yuck."

"If it doesn't work, I'll blame you. Poor data quality."

"Ha ha. Why do you get to do all the fun stuff, while I slave away cleaning data for your precious algorithms?"

"It's not my fault you majored in statistics."

Emma elbowed him. "Take that."

They started to make out, but suddenly Arvind stopped and fumbled for his phone.

"Huh? What are you doing?" said Emma.

"Filling out the consent form."

"Seriously? You're such a goody two shoes. No one files those things any more. But noo, you still have to do it every time."

"Well, if I don't, we could get a visit from the Guards."

"Nah. Unlikely."

"Better safe than sorry."

"Fucking bureaucracy."

"Yeah, they should name it that. The Office of Fucking Bureaucracy. Er . . . are we planning to have oral sex tonight?"

Emma rolled her eyes. "I'm not in the mood anymore."

The local news came on. "A truck flipped over earlier this evening at the intersection of Van Ness and California," said the anchor. The TV cut to footage of the truck being pulled back upright with a boom and hooks extended from a rescue vehicle.

"Wow, look at that," said Emma.

"Reports say the truck was being driven by Ethan Burnswagger, former CEO of KumbAI."

"What?!" Arvind jumped up and sat on the edge of the couch, watching intently.

"Bree Porter is on the scene," said the anchor.

Cut to the reporter interviewing a Guard.

"We'll find the son of a bitch," said the Guard.

"Do you think he's OK?" Emma said.

"Let me call him." He tapped Ethan's number on his

phone, but got the voice mail prompt.

"Hey Ethan, Arvind here. Just saw your accident on the news. Are you OK? Call me."

"Why was Ethan driving a truck at night on Van Ness?"

"Beats me."

"We have in the studio Professor Dayna Sauer of the Institute for Imaginary Injustice," said the anchor. "Professor, these incidents seem to be on the rise. What's your explanation?"

"This is yet another rich white boy who thinks our city is his playground," said Prof. Sauer. "Think of how much distress he's caused the marginalized communities in the Brown sector. We need to pre-emptively detain these privileged pigs of the patriarchy."

Suddenly they heard the sound of their first-floor studio apartment's electronic door lock opening.

"Aaah! Burglar! Call the Guards!" screamed Emma.

"Good luck with that," said Arvind, getting up.

The door opened and a man wearing an orange uniform with the Zero Click logo appeared.

"Oh—sorry, I'll be back later," he said. "There's usually no one home at this hour. Sorry."

"No, no, please come in," said Arvind. "We're fine."

They scrambled to compose themselves while the Zero-Click guy restocked the refrigerator.

A commercial break came on. An army of PresiBots rampaged through an American city, killing, stomping on dead bodies, blowing up cars and buildings, more and more descending from the sky on jets and wings. Finally they marched across the obliterated town and toward the camera, thump,

thump, thump. "Today PresiBot, tomorrow Terminator," said the voice-over. "Only Raging Bull can save us."

"This is so absurd," said Arvind.

"But it's going to do a lot of damage," said Emma. "We need to come up with a counter."

The Zero-Click guy had stopped restocking the refrigerator to watch the ad.

"So who you gonna vote for?" asked Emma.

"Well, if it's a choice between ending America and ending humanity, I'd rather just end America," he said, resuming the restocking.

When he was done, he apologized again and left, carefully closing the door.

They started making out again. Arvind tried to remember if he'd filed the consent form. Suddenly Emma screamed and pointed to the window. "There's a man there!"

Arvind turned and squinted.

The man in the window knocked. "Please open!" he said, muffled by the glass.

Arvind went closer. "Ethan, is that you?"

"Yes!"

Arvind opened the window and Ethan clambered in. At the last moment he tripped on the sill and fell flat on the floor. "Story of my life," he mumbled. He sat on the floor and looked up. "Sorry, am I interrupting something?"

Arvind sighed. "No, not really."

"Sorry for coming in like this," Ethan said, looking for a chair and pulling one up from the kitchen table. "I'd rather not be seen right now."

"Look at you!" said Emma. "You're all bruised! And your

clothes are all torn!"

Ethan shrugged.

"What happened?" asked Arvind.

"Long story."

"You need to take care of yourself," said Emma, still looking him up and down. "Arvind can lend you some clothes. Right, Arvind?"

"Sure," said Arvind.

"Not sure they'll fit, though," said Ethan.

"Come," said Emma.

She grabbed a T-shirt and jeans from the closet and motioned Ethan to the bathroom. "Now put these on."

Ethan nodded, pulled off the shreds of his T-shirt and struggled into Arvind's.

"You do look like you're about to burst out of that T-shirt," giggled Emma.

Ethan shrugged, as if to say it wasn't his fault he was so ripped.

"Wow, look at those muscles," said Emma, putting her hand on his biceps.

Their eyes locked.

"Now, now," said Ethan.

Emma sighed.

"—your complete home security solution! With free burglar prediction—" blared the TV. Emma left him to finish changing. When he emerged, they looked at him with frank curiosity.

"Well, tell us," said Arvind.

"I've found the panic button."

"Wow, that's a relief!" said Emma. "Where was it?"

"In a garbage truck. In fact, I spent the last several hours desperately trying to keep it from falling into the wrong hands."

"So that's what that was," Arvind said.

"But then it dawned on me."

"What did?"

"Why not let them have it?"

"Huh?"

"Let everyone have their own panic button."

Arvind and Emma looked at him uncomprehendingly.

"Crowdsource PresiBot," Ethan said.

"Ha," said Emma.

"That's insane," said Arvind.

"Hear me out," said Ethan. "We need to get people more engaged—it's all about engagement—so how do we do that? We give them an app that lets them control PresiBot."

"But that's chaos," said Arvind. "How can they all control PresiBot at the same time?"

"They don't. PresiBot just listens to them and decides what to do. In real time. No flesh-and-blood politician can match that. People will love it."

"Some people," said Emma. "Most won't care."

"We can use all the usual gimmicks to get them engaged. And they'll feel rewarded when PresiBot does something they want. We can get them addicted—you rule the country!"

"That sounds like a very dangerous idea," said Arvind. "And it's not technically feasible, anyway."

"Why not?"

"Wake up, Ethan. We're weeks from the election. Who's going to implement the app and the new version of PresiBot, test them, and debug them in time to win the election? Completely impossible."

"Not really."

"How?"

"Most of PresiBot doesn't need to change. It's just that the input is now coming from live people instead of historical data. Think how much better that will be! PresiBot drawing on the real-time intelligence of millions of people, instead of just mining old—"

"That's what I'm afraid of," said Arvind.

"Real-time democracy! Think about it! Real—time—democracy! For the first time in history!"

Arvind shook his head. "Mob rule, is more like it."

"No, because the AI is still running the show. It just takes continuous input from the people, as any leader should."

"Even if we could do that, we don't have time to build the app."

"That's the best part. The app is just the panic button with a slightly modified interface. Like, instead of 'DON'T PANIC', it can say 'RULE THE WORLD!'"

"I think you're insane," said Arvind. "Did you get a concussion from that truck accident?"

"Ha," said Ethan. "I did, as a matter of fact, but never mind that now."

"Well, actually," said Emma, "maybe this is not such a bad idea."

"You too?" said Arvind, turning to her.

"Look, we're going to lose the election big time unless we do something," she said. "This sounds like something. You have a better idea?"

2040: A SILICON VALLEY SATIRE

Arvind hesitated. "We don't know what we're getting into."

"But then again, we didn't either when we decided to do PresiBot," Emma said. "And this will destroy Raging Bull's attack line that PresiBot is the robot takeover."

Arvind hesitated some more.

"If this works, every company will want to have it," said Ethan. "But we can't do it without you."

"We? You're not even part of KumbAI anymore."

"I think Newald will like this idea. It's right up his alley. Besides, I have the panic button. If he doesn't reinstate me, I pull the plug on PresiBot."

"And go to jail."

"Try me."

"We'd love to have you back, of course," Arvind said.

"Make sure you tell him that."

Arvind was silent for a while. "Anyway, there's another reason this is not feasible," he said finally.

"What's that?" Ethan said.

"There's no way in hell we can get it to work in real time."

"Why not? PresiBot already works in real time, and the rest is just a large amount of speech recognition and data preprocessing."

"Yes, but it needs to be done in fractions of a second. How're you gonna pull that off?"

"It's all embarrassingly parallel until it gets to combining the inputs, which PresiBot already does. Trivial."

Arvind sighed. "We're going to need a bigger data center."

11

PRESIBOT 2.0

PresiBot stood perfectly still at a lectern in the middle of a rented TV studio, flanked by American flags, not sweating at all in the intense glare of the lights. Above it, a wall-size display showed a stylized map of the United States and various statistics, topped by the title "All America Town Hall". In the control room, panic was rising.

"I don't know why PresiBot is not working," said Arvind.

"Come on, there's seven million people waiting," said Ethan.

"More like six now," said Emma. "People are leaving."

"We're almost an hour late," said Rossi. "Might as well call off the whole thing."

"We should have gone full virtual," said Emma. "None of this crap to deal with."

"Not the same," said Ethan.

Arvind stared intently at his laptop's screen.

"Ah, I think I've found the bug."

"Fix it! Fix it!" said Ethan.

Arvind typed a few things, waited for the system build to finish, and then looked up at PresiBot.

Nothing.

"No, that wasn't it. Let me undo."

"No time! Hurry up!"

"Maybe it's a hardware problem."

"Great!"

"Actually, turn off the lights."

"OK," said the technician, and the studio plunged into darkness.

Arvind typed a PresiBot command into his laptop.

"Is PresiBot moving?" he asked.

"I don't know, I can't see it," Ethan said.

"Wait—I hear the whirring!" Emma said.

Ethan ran up to the robot with his cell phone light.

"Yess! PresiBot has raised its hand to greet the crowd!"

"I knew it!" said Arvind. "It's the power LED circuitry in the studio. Interferes with the link."

"Seriously?" said Ethan.

"Never mind that now!" said Emma. "Start the show!"

"But we have no lights," said the director. "The cameras are blind."

"Shoot!" said Ethan.

"No, we can't shoot," said the director.

"Do you have any, er, non-electronic lights?" said Arvind.

"Nope," said the director.

"I think we have an old klieg light in the closet," said the engineer.

The director looked at him blankly.

"You know, for the classic movie look. Haven't used it in a looong time."

"OK, get it," said the director. "Hurry up!"

PRESIBOT 2.0

Three minutes and 27 seconds later, the klieg light was shining brightly, if somewhat unsteadily, on PresiBot.

"Start!" said Ethan. "Go go go!"

PresiBot raised its hand again to greet the people.

"Here we go," said Rossi. "PresiBot directly interacting with five million people. Hope it works."

"Or rather, five million people interacting with each other through PresiBot," said Ethan.

"People of America!" boomed PresiBot. "Ask me anything!"

Silence.

"What's wrong?" Ethan said.

"Nothing," Arvind said. "It's processing. Look at the counts."

Over each state on the display, a counter showed the number of questions coming from it, and they were all going up rapidly. Finally they stopped.

"Too much dead time," Ethan muttered.

"It'll be instantaneous once the predictive responses kick in," Arvind said.

"What's that?" asked Rossi.

"PresiBot's large language model can finish people's sentences ahead of them."

"And as the first question asker, I've chosen . . . Brenda Wilson, of Tampa, Florida!" announced PresiBot. The display zoomed into Florida, then Tampa, then Brenda's video stream—blonde, thirtyish, heavy makeup—now being shown to everyone in the virtual town hall. In the control room, the borrowed Happinet emotion meters sitting next to the mixing console zoomed to her readings, equal parts nervousness and giddy pride.

"Brenda, what do you do?"

"I'm a waitress at Burger Slurper and mother of three."

"Thank you! And what is your question?"

"How will I make ends meet?"

"Very important question! Now everyone, give me your answers, and I'll synthesize mine from them!"

"That's an odd one to pick," Emma said.

Arvind shrugged. The display changed to a mosaic of voters talking to their phones in selfie position, their voices an immense cacophony, building and crashing like an ocean wave. The Happinet meters showed a mix of boredom and excitement.

"Here's the answer!" said PresiBot, and paused. "Are you ready, Brenda?"

Brenda nodded.

"Quit Burger Slurper! Jules et Jim's on Kennedy has openings for waitresses and pays much better!"

"Oh, thank you so much!" she said.

"You're welcome! Next question! John Chen of Philadelphia, Pennsylvania!"

"How are you going to turn your campaign around?" asked John.

"And the answer iiiiis . . . you, the people, will turn it around for me! Talk to your friends, family members, and coworkers! Convince them to reject Raging Bull! Donate what you can and volunteer at PresiVote.com! I'm counting on you!"

Loud cheering.

"Next! Linda Blackbird Howe of Puyallup, Washington!"

"How will you bring more revenue to Indian reservations?"

"Open stock markets there!"

More cheering.

"Next!"

"How will you make health care affordable?"

"I won't! It's an unfixable problem! I'd be lying to you if I told you otherwise!"

Disappointment, turning into respect for PresiBot's honesty.

The questions kept coming.

"Why haven't we heard anything about your running mate?"

"Because it's just a backup copy of me!"

"What do you think of Joe Blur?"

"He's an insult to the American people! You don't pick a random middle-aged white man as your running mate just to show how inclusive you are! What was Raging Bull thinking?"

"Should Supreme Court justices be AIs?"

"Yes, of course!"

"But how will you maintain the separation of powers if they're all you?"

"They won't be! One will be a Bayesian network, another a genetic algorithm, and so on!"

"Why do you want to be president?"

"I don't want anything! I'm just an algorithm for combining your views and preferences into executive decisions!"

"How will you make America great again?"

"Wrong question! The right question is . . ."

"How will we make America great again?"

"Correct! And the answer is?"

"By working closer together!"

"Loving thy neighbor!"

"Singing in the shower!"

After almost an hour of this, PresiBot raised its hand again.

"People of America, thank you for participating!" it said, and waited for the nationwide chatter to die down. "Before you go, I have some questions of my own for you. Did you like this All America Town Hall?"

"Loved it!"

"Do you feel empowered?"

"Yess!"

"Will you vote for me?"

"Yes! Yes! Yes!"

"What should my campaign slogan be?"

"Let the people govern!"

PresiBot raised its fist. "Say it with me: Let the people govern! Let the people govern! Let the people govern!"

The chant of five million voices poured forth from the speakers. Finally PresiBot opened its arms as if embracing the whole nation, and the chant dissolved into a wave of applause.

"Good night, and God bless America!" said PresiBot.

Finally PresiBot was silent, and the display switched to a summary of the nationwide Happinet meter readings.

"Wow," said Ethan, looking at them. "That seems to have worked."

"Yeah, these readings are almost as good as after a live rally," said Rossi. "But with a thousand times more people."

"Only PresiBot could do a town hall in every town at once and not be overwhelmed," said Ethan.

"What an efficient way to run a campaign," marveled

Rossi. "I think we're on to something here."

"This, my friends, is the future of politics," said Ethan.

"You know what's interesting?" said Emma. "I was looking at PresiBot's internal logs, and it did a lot less processing than we expected."

"How's that?" asked Arvind.

"It barely did any combination of answers. Mostly just picked one from someone."

"Sounded like it," said Arvind.

"It figures," said Ethan. "With millions of answers to choose from, there's always at least one good one."

"I don't know about good," said Arvind. "Open stock markets in the reservations?"

"The people liked it," said Emma.

"Well, if that's the standard . . ." said Arvind. "But I'm sure PresiBot 1.0 would have come up with something much more sensible."

"Doesn't matter," said Ethan. "Democracy is about winning votes."

"Speaking of which, the instapolls are already climbing," said Rossi, looking at his laptop. "If they keep going like this, we'll be in good shape."

Panic and chaos reigned in Raging Bull's teepee at the Glassman Hotel.

"How could they make a huge change like this so late in the campaign?" said Valerie White, the campaign's chief strategist.

"It's the AI," said Max Bloomstein, the field director. "It doesn't work like a normal politician. We're screwed."

"Where's your Robopocalypse now?" said Raging Bull venomously to Naomi Jackson. "Why did we waste so much money on your stupid ads?"

"Folks, calm down," said Jackson. "None of this matters now."

"Oh really?" Raging Bull said.

"I just received a leak from PresiBot's campaign."

Raging Bull looked at her with raised eyebrows.

"A leak that will put an end to it once and for all."

Expectant silence.

"KumbAI has been acquired by Happinet. Dave Newald now owns PresiBot."

Stunned silence.

Raging Bull whistled.

"No—fucking—way," said Bloomstein.

"That can't be legal!" said White.

"We'll see," said Jackson. "But either way, once we leak this to the media, PresiBot is history."

"I told you!" yelled Raging Bull. "PresiBot was Newald's tool all along!"

"I don't know about that," said Jackson. "This new version seems to be all about channeling the people."

"Hah! Anyone can see through that! It's just a trick—it says what it wants, and makes them think—"

"Pretty clever, actually," said Jackson.

"Why the fuck did I ever listen to you? We should have gone all out for the plutocracy's-puppet angle from day one!"

"Luckily, there's still time to fix that. We're going to blitz them with a pile of attack ads they'll never recover from."

"Like one with Newald physically pulling PresiBot's strings," said White.

"Or a spoof of a PresiBot ad laying out his pro-rich agenda and ending with Newald saying 'I'm Dave Newald and I approve of this message,'" said Bloomstein.

"Hell, they're doomed even if we don't do anything," said Jackson. "This thing will snowball out of anyone's control."

"Wow," said White. "They nearly had us."

"So that's how they were able to pull off that stunt last night," said Bloomstein. "Happinet's technology."

"It's really going to cost them now," said Jackson.

"I was right! I was right, dammit!" yelled Raging Bull. "Your Robopocalypse bullshit nearly cost me the election!"

"Don't get carried away, John. There's still—"

"It's time to unplug that tin can once and for all." He picked up his AK-47 from the floor and started loading it, then looked around at his acolytes. "Rock and roll, my braves, I mean, lock and load. I have a mission for you."

Jackson gazed at him with growing alarm. "John, the stress of the campaign is getting to you. Have you been doing your yoga? Maybe you should up the dosage on your meds until it's over, just to be safe."

"To hell with that! I am Chief Raging Bull of the Lakota, and the avenger of every crime the wasichu have ever perpetrated on us Native Americans! Death to the colonists! No more yoga! Enough of your attempts to control me!"

"John—"

"I'm done listening to you. You're lucky I don't fire you right this moment. From now on we'll just do as I say. Let's go."

Ethan glared at the image of Rossi on his phone. "Did you do it?" he asked.

"Of course not!" Rossi said. "Why on Earth would I?"

"So what are these rumors I've heard of you hanging out with Naomi Jackson?"

Rossi blushed. "I haven't been hanging out with her! I just ran into her in DC a week ago, and talked with her some. Nothing wrong with that."

"So that's all it was?"

"I— I—" Rossi stammered. "Look, it could have been anyone. One of your people, probably."

"Oh yeah? Why would anyone at KumbAI do it? To make sure the DOJ blocks the acquisition and they go back to being poor?"

"I know, I know. It doesn't make any sense."

"So?"

"Look, it doesn't matter now. We'll turn this around."

"Oh yeah? How? Everyone says we're done for."

"No, everyone says next week's debate will be our last stand."

"What's the difference?"

"We can still pull something at the debate."

"Like what?"

"I don't know. You're the AI guy. What other tricks can PresiBot do? That town hall was really something. And it worked— until— until—"

Ethan looked at Rossi. "You're right. There is something we can do."

"Yess! What is it?"

"We can take it to the next level."

"How?"

"We'll have PresiBot *be* the people. Just repeat what one of them says into PresiApp as they watch. Let *them* debate Raging Bull."

"Whoa. That sounds a little dangerous."

"Think about it. What better way to kill off the whole 'PresiBot is Newald's tool' line of attack than have it literally be the voice of the voters?"

"But people will say stupid things. Things that could sink PresiBot."

"That's what the AI is there for. There'll be millions of answers to choose from. We already know it works. Best of all, the people will love it. They'll feel even more empowered. It's a win-win."

Rossi nodded. "But can you pull it off? There's less than a week left."

"Sure, why not? It's the same system we already have, just used in a slightly different way. Besides, what's to lose?"

"True."

"Never underestimate KumbAI."

12

THE MACHINE ROOM
WHERE IT HAPPENS

Ethan, Arvind, Emma and PresiBot got out of the Secret Service robocar and walked into the Moscone Convention Center, a few blocks from the Flower.

"I have a bad feeling about this," said Arvind.

"Relax," said Ethan. "We'll be fine. And worst case, I still have the panic button. Right here in my pocket."

"But we didn't have time to test anything," said Arvind.

"This debate is the only test we'll need. Now which way—"

"Hi," said a shapely young woman in a tight minidress. "Are you Ethan Burnswagger?"

"Very much so," said Ethan, eyes on her cleavage.

"I'll be your minder today," she said with a welcoming smile. "My name is Pandora Swift. Please follow me to the green room."

They walked past the main hall and down a corridor.

"What are you doing after the debate?" Ethan asked, glancing over his shoulder at her.

"Having drinks with you," she said, touching his arm.

"It's a date," said Ethan.

"Founder hounder alert," muttered Arvind. Emma rolled her eyes.

Pandora opened the green room's door for them. "Make yourselves at home," she said.

"I'll go set up PresiBot onstage," said Arvind.

"Roger that," said Ethan. "I'll check the connection to the Flower's data center on my laptop."

Arvind left with PresiBot. Ethan sat down on one of the chairs and opened his laptop, but couldn't help glancing up at Pandora and eavesdropping on her as she chatted with Emma.

"Wow, that guy is hot," Pandora said, nodding toward Ethan.

Emma gave her a dirty look.

"Is he your boyfriend?"

"No," Emma said, biting her lip.

"Not in your league, huh?"

"Shut up, bitch."

"I think I'll take him home tonight," Pandora said. She came over toward Ethan and put her arm around him. "Are you comfy, dear?" she whispered in his ear.

"Never better," said Ethan, locking eyes with her.

She gave him a quick kiss on the lips. "I'll be back when it's time," she said, and sashayed out the door.

"Come here, Ethan," said Emma. Pushing his laptop away, she started furiously kissing him. *Whoa*, thought Ethan, dazed. She sat on his lap, heaving, pulling him toward her, and the kiss got deeper. He could feel her breasts tight against his chest, their tongues locked in a mad dance, and . . .

The door opened, and Arvind was standing there, a USB cable in his hand, a look of horror and pain on his face.

"Wait—" Ethan said, trying to push Emma away.

"What?" said Emma. She turned around and froze.

Arvind turned and ran out of the room.

"Arvind!" yelled Ethan. "Wait!"

Emma frantically tried to compose herself. "Oh my god . . . What have we done?"

Ethan ran out after Arvind. Where was he? There, halfway down the corridor. Ethan caught up with him and blocked his way, panting.

"Go away! Go away!" Arvind yelled.

"I'm so sorry. I really am."

"You son of a bitch! How could you do that?"

"It was her, I swear."

Arvind tried to punch him, but Ethan grabbed his wrist. "Calm down," he said. "We have bigger things to worry about. We can sort this out later."

Arvind freed himself and started running the other way.

"Arvind!" said Emma as he came barreling down the corridor. "I'm—"

"Get out of my way!" he cried, dodging her. "I never want to see you again!"

They chased him all the way to the street. He jumped into one of the waiting robocabs and locked the door. "Drive!"

"Arvind!" Ethan begged, banging on the window. "Don't go! We need you here!"

"I'll show you," said Arvind, and sped away.

Ethan and Emma looked at each other as the car disappeared in the traffic.

"Now we've done it," said Ethan.

"This is all my fault," said Emma, and started sobbing.

"It's OK," said Ethan, putting his arm around her. "We'll iron it all out. One thing at a time. Let's go check on PresiBot."

They went into the main hall and climbed onstage. PresiBot stood impassively by its lectern. People were starting to filter in. Ethan went to get his laptop from the green room, hooked it up to PresiBot and ran the full suite of diagnostics.

"Well, it's ready to go," he said to Emma. "At least we don't have to worry about that."

They went back to the green room and waited in silence. Thoughts and worries raced through Ethan's head. What could go wrong now? What was Arvind going to do? Finally Pandora came to get them.

"What's wrong?" she said.

"Nothing," said Ethan.

The auditorium was packed, Raging Bull on stage with his AK-47 slung over his shoulder, the front rows filled with his henchmen in Lakota garb and staffers from both campaigns, Naomi Jackson looking at her watch.

"Hi," said Vince Rossi as they sat down next to him. "Where's Arvind?"

"Long story," said Ethan. "Won't be joining us today."

"Is everything OK?" asked Rossi.

"I hope so. We'll see."

After what seemed like an interminable time, the lights dimmed and the countdown flashed on the screen above the stage.

"Good evening, and welcome to the second and final

debate of the 2040 presidential election," said the moderator from her desk at the foot of the stage. "I'm Roshanda Williams from the Black Broadcasting Corporation, and we are live from the Moscone Center in San Francisco."

PresiBot went through its opening statement, but Ethan was distracted and missed most of it.

"Chief Bull, your turn," said Williams.

"First of all, I thank the Ohlone for their hospitality," started Raging Bull. "And I promise the white occupation will soon be over."

His warriors and half the audience erupted in cheers. Ethan's attention drifted again.

"Mn. PresiBot," said Williams, "who will really be president if you're elected?"

Now it begins, thought Ethan.

"The American people," said PresiBot.

"Enough of your lies, Head in the Cloud!" thundered Raging Bull. "Why are you standing there? It should be Dave Newald. Enough of the puppet! Let's see the puppet master!"

"I don't work for Dave Newald."

"But you do! We all know you do! The jig is up!"

"Just because KumbAI is a subsidiary of Happinet doesn't mean Newald controls me."

"Prove it!"

"KumbAI's deal with Happinet specifically disallows interfering with my operation."

"You expect us to believe that?"

"The documents are now public."

"You expect us to believe some piece of paper? You think we're stupid?"

"You may not believe in U.S. federal law, but I do."

Good one, thought Ethan. *I wonder who came up with that.* He stole a glance at the Happinet meters on his laptop. *Looking good.*

"People! Good people!" said Raging Bull. "Happinet just bought the next president of the United States—if you vote for it. But you won't, will you?"

"No, Chief," said PresiBot. "Happinet didn't buy me, because I am the people, and the people can't be bought."

Loud cheering from PresiBot's side of the audience.

"You're not the people," scoffed Raging Bull. "You're just a robot in a suit."

"And you are—"

"OK, OK," said Williams. "Chief, what will you do with the U.S. Army?"

"Disband it, of course," said Raging Bull. "They're the worst."

"But the U.S. military saved the world from the Nazis," said Williams.

"There are no Nazis to save the world from now."

"No, just you," said PresiBot.

"So I'm disbanding them," said Raging Bull. "Take that."

"No," said PresiBot. "We the people don't want our military disbanded. It stays."

So far so good, thought Ethan. He glanced at the Happinet meters again. *Wow! The people are loving it!*

"You see this?" said Raging Bull. "Head in the Cloud wants to keep things just as they are, because that serves its masters just fine. Why should the rich and privileged want anything to change?"

THE MACHINE ROOM WHERE IT HAPPENS

"Oh, I'll change plenty," said PresiBot. "I'll abolish the Community Guards, for starters."

Wow! Where did that come from? The meters— *Yeah! Off the charts!*

"But you don't have the legal authority to do that!"

"Since when do you care about legal authority? When it suits you?"

Yeah, thought Ethan. *Go people!*

"Ha! You're the one who wants to keep America!" said Raging Bull. "I want something better!"

"Yes, you want to be a dictator."

"Not true!"

"Slow down, folks," said Williams. "I'm supposed to be running this show." She paused. "Mn. PresiBot, how can you guarantee that your new crowdsourced version won't lead to a disaster? Or that your next version won't be something totally different from what people voted for?"

"Well, obviously—" started PresiBot, but suddenly froze. Everyone waited expectantly. "Reboot in progress," said PresiBot in a tinny computer voice.

No! Noo! What the hell is going on? Ethan typed frantically into his laptop, but PresiBot was offline. A hundred million viewers waited while the robot stood completely immobile on stage.

"Mn. PresiBot, can you hear me?" asked Williams.

Nothing.

Ethan tapped Arvind's number on his phone, but no luck. He tried Granite—no luck either.

"PresiBot is not responding," said Williams. "Chief, would you like to say something while we wait for it to reboot?"

"This is exactly why we shouldn't make a machine president!" said Raging Bull triumphantly. "What if the bot breaks down during a national emergency? What if it malfunctions and starts a nuclear war?"

"Downloading system version 1.0," said the tinny voice coming from PresiBot.

Ethan and Emma looked at each other.

"What the fuck?" whispered Emma.

"I know what happened," said Ethan suddenly. "This is Arvind's doing. He's switched PresiBot back to 1.0. Son of a bitch!"

"No fucking way."

"I'm telling you. He never liked 2.0, and now he's getting back at us."

"But how? It's locked for the duration of the debate. No one can access it."

"He must be in the Flower's data center, hooking directly into the servers."

"Yikes!"

Up on stage, PresiBot suddenly came to life and regurgitated its opening statement from the first debate.

Think, thought Ethan. *Think.*

"Mn. PresiBot, what just happened?" Williams asked.

"What do you mean?" PresiBot asked back.

"Why did you just reboot?"

PresiBot processed for a moment. "Let's get on with the debate," it finally said. "Why don't you ask me another question?"

"OK," said Williams. "Will your cabinet be composed of AIs?"

"I'm going to run to the Flower," whispered Ethan, "and see if I can fix this."

Emma nodded. "Hurry."

Ethan got up and sprinted down the side aisle, head down, and then across the lobby and out to the street. He dashed across Third Street in the traffic, dodging cars and furious honking, and raced up Howard, zigzagging through the crowd.

"What the fuck?" he heard someone say. "PresiApp isn't working!"

"Mine neither," said another voice. "It's been sabotaged!"

"It's Happinet! They've unplugged us!"

"It's Newald—he doesn't want us controlling PresiBot!"

"Fucker! He'd rather control us!"

Ethan swerved left at Howard and Beale and faced an even denser crowd. Irate people were coming out of the buildings and congregating on the street, yelling, gesticulating, egging each other on.

"What the hell?"

"I'm not going to take this anymore!"

"We want PresiBot back, Newald!"

"I am PresiBot!"

The shouts grew louder, the mob thickening and drifting toward the Flower. Someone smashed a shop window, then another. Ethan jumped into the middle of the street to avoid the crowd and started running down the center-line, cars swerving and grazing him left and right. There—Market Street—Protest Plaza, overflowing with a crowd chanting "I am PresiBot! I am PresiBot!"—the Flower. Ethan burst into the lobby and ran toward the elevators.

"Sir!" said a Secret Service agent, blocking his way. "This area is off limits!"

"What do you mean, off limits?"

"Access is restricted while the data center houses PresiBot."

"Let me in, then! I'm the CEO of KumbAI!"

"Do you have a Security Pass?"

"No, I don't have a Security Pass! This is urgent!"

"Sorry, sir, we can't let you in, then."

Ethan pulled up his ID on his phone. "Look! I'm Ethan Burnswagger! Now will you let me in?"

"Sorry, sir. Only authorized personnel."

Ethan had an idea. He looked for a picture of Arvind on his phone and showed it to the agent. "Did you recently see this person?"

"Sorry, I can't tell you."

"Come on! He's my CTO!"

"Please leave now."

"Listen to me! This guy is trying to sabotage PresiBot! You have to help me stop him! It's *your* head if you screw this up!"

The agent hesitated for a moment. "OK, yes. He went down to the data center."

"Aaargh!" cried Ethan. "Did he have a Security Pass?"

"Yes, of course."

Ethan looked frantically around him. *How do I get down there?* Two more agents were converging on him.

"What's the matter here, Jones?" said the older one.

"This guy says he's the CEO of KumbAI, Captain Thompson, sir," said Jones, "and that there's a sabotage of PresiBot in progress."

"I was wondering what that hooha at the debate was," Thompson said. "What do you know?" he asked Ethan.

"My CTO has gone rogue and reverted PresiBot to an earlier version without permission. We need to restore it—now, now, now."

"Let's go down there and sort this out. Jones, Smith, come with us. Radio Baker to replace you."

They got in the elevator. "It's a big data center," said Thompson. "Do you know where your colleague might be?"

"By whichever server PresiBot 1.0 was uploaded to," said Ethan, "if he's still there."

"And which one is that?"

"We need to find out."

The elevator doors opened, and they stepped out. Ethan tried to get his bearings in the dim light, amid the deafening roar of the data center's giant fan. Walking around it, looking down each server corridor, he suddenly saw Arvind a hundred feet away, laptop plugged into a server, typing.

"Arvind! Stop!" Ethan cried, running toward him.

Arvind looked up and blanched. In a flash he was running, laptop in hand, Ethernet cable trailing behind him.

"Get him! Get him!" Ethan yelled to the agents behind him. But at the next intersection Arvind darted to the left, and when Ethan got there he had disappeared.

Standing in the Flower's control room, surrounded by his troops, Newald watched the situation across the country unfold. A meme that Happinet had sabotaged PresiBot had gone viral, and the anger, spilling into the red in every meter no matter how you sliced and diced it, was like lava pouring out of the ground.

"Why isn't the content block working?" he asked Kah Xing, his Chief Happiness Officer.

"The meme is mutating too fast. By the time we block something, there's already ten other versions out there."

"What about the mood waves? Send these people calm, depression, I don't care."

"Not enough. Most of them aren't even on their phones right now. They're on the street, yelling and smashing things up. We can't influence them. Even the ones we can, it's not enough. They're too angry."

"Come on, there must be something we can do. What does the optimizer say?"

"It's confused. This situation is an outlier. It doesn't have enough data to know what to do."

Newald cursed under his breath. Just then his phone rang, and he picked up. "Hello?"

"Dave? This is Thomas Monk."

"Oh hi, Thomas. What's up?"

"I'm in Tibet."

"Aha."

"In a monastery."

"Right. Have you seen what's happening over here?"

"No."

"Good for you. Stay in Tibet, is my advice."

"There's something I need to tell you . . . not sure how."

"Just say it."

"Fate's book is open on your page."

"Huh?"

"I've been studying fate's book . . . in the sky. It has billions of pages . . . one for every one of us. And when your time comes, it opens on your page."

"You're not making any sense."

"Dave, it's open on your page now."

"And what am I supposed to do about it?"

"I don't know, but there's something else . . ."

"OK, what is it?"

"I saw a great tsunami enveloping the Flower."

"That seems unlikely. We have the Golden Gate Dam now."

"Yes, but the tsunami was coming from inland."

"From inland? That doesn't make any sense."

"I know, I know, but I keep seeing it . . . I don't know what it means . . . but watch out."

"OK, Thomas, thanks for the heads up." Pause. "Gotta go now. Have fun in Lhasa, or wherever you are."

"Take care, Dave."

Newald hung up and was silent for a moment. Then he went back to looking at the monitors. Hector, his head of security, emerged from the elevator and came jogging up to him. "Sir, there's a very large crowd forming in Protest Plaza," he said.

"Bigger than usual?"

"Way bigger. Overflows up and down Market Street. And they're packed like sardines."

Ethan ran past one corridor after another, looking down each one, trying to spot Arvind. There! Someone darting away at the end! With a desperate surge, he bounded down the corridor, turned the corner and—bam!—ran head-on into someone and fell over them in a confusion of limbs and curses.

"What the—? You're not Arvind!"

"Get off me, asshole! Get off!"

Ethan rolled off the man and scrambled to his feet. So did the man, and suddenly they recognized each other.

"You're . . . that guy! The spy!" said the man.

"José!"

The agents pulled out their guns and pointed them at José.

"Don't move," said Thompson.

"OK, OK," said José. He eyed Ethan resentfully. "I knew you were a spy!"

"Where's Arvind?" asked Ethan.

"Who?"

"The Indian guy I was running after."

"Oh, that one! Yeah, we got him. Uh huh."

"Who's we?" asked Thompson.

"You have to let me go," said José. "If you let me go, I'll bring him to you, I swear."

"Very funny," said Ethan.

"Who's we?" asked Thompson again.

"Look, you guys are toast anyway," said Ethan. "But if you cooperate, you might get some leniency."

José considered this. Then he sighed. "Gibbon! Bring the guy!" he yelled over his shoulder.

Gibbon and Arvind emerged from behind a row of servers, Gibbon holding a knife to Arvind's throat. Arvind gave

Ethan a resentful look.

"Arvind! Come to your senses!" said Ethan. "Let's reinstall PresiBot 2.0 ASAP and put all this behind us!"

"Do it yourself, Mr. CEO," said Arvind.

"You know I can't. I don't know how you bypassed the boot lock."

"Not my problem. Figure it out."

"Well, I got this," said Ethan, taking the panic button out of his pocket.

"Use it. See if I care."

"You have to care! PresiBot is your baby as much as mine!"

"PresiBot is a monstrosity, and we should never have made it."

Ethan considered Arvind for a moment. "It was you who leaked the acquisition, wasn't it? I should have known."

"Someone needed to. People deserve to know."

"But you've handed the election to Raging Bull!"

"It's better this way."

"How can you say that? After all the work we've put into it? It's the end of KumbAI!"

"Let it be. All is karma."

"You rebooted PresiBot?" asked Gibbon, who had followed the exchange with keen interest. "What's wrong with you, man? It was kicking butt until you ruined it."

"You've been watching the debate?" Ethan asked.

Gibbon nodded and tapped the display over his eye. "I got PresiApp too, man, but now it's not working. Sucks."

"You see?" Ethan said to Arvind. "There's millions like him. Let them be heard for once!"

Arvind shrugged. Ethan considered the panic button in

his hand. Yes or no? Could he do better than PresiBot 1.0? What's to lose?

"What you got there?" Gibbon asked. "Some kind of remote for PresiBot?"

Suddenly José slipped behind Gibbon and bolted down a side corridor. "Jones! After him!" yelled Thompson. Jones scrambled to it, but bumped into Gibbon's shoulder, throwing him off balance. Arvind saw his chance and bolted in the opposite direction. Ethan ran after him, down one corridor, right, down another, left— Suddenly Arvind stopped, and Ethan screeched to a halt right behind him. In front of them were a dozen of Raging Bull's men, AK-47s pointed at them.

"What the hell—?" Ethan said.

The warrior in front put a finger to his lips.

Ethan's mind raced. *They must have broken into a vent. And they're here to sabotage PresiBot.*

"Listen, brave ones," said Arvind steadily. "This guy has a device that can disable PresiBot." He nodded toward Ethan. "All you have to do is take it from him."

The warrior shoved the barrel of his AK-47 into Ethan's chest and put out his hand. "Now."

Damn. Ethan reluctantly took the panic button from his pocket and extended it to the warrior—it touched his hand—Ethan let go—

That moment Thompson and Smith came running around the corner, panting, guns in hand. One of the warriors fired his AK-47 and everyone dropped to the ground. The panic button slid under a row of servers. Gibbon, watching from the corner, saw it and ran down the next corridor to the spot as more shots rang out. He felt under the servers with his hand, pulled out the panic button, and ran.

Finally he stopped and leaned against a server rack. Turning on the panic button, he looked down at the screen and saw it was just like PresiApp.

The debate was still playing in his ears. "I'm the Lakota avenger!" said Raging Bull.

With a mad glow in his eyes, Gibbon pushed the button and raised it to his lips.

13

THE AMERICAN SCREAM

Emma shifted anxiously in her seat. Where was Ethan? And when was he going to switch PresiBot back to 2.0?

"I'm the Lakota avenger!" said Raging Bull onstage, pounding the lectern.

"The hell you are!" said PresiBot, channeling Gibbon. "You're just a small-time influencer who got carried away with his impersonation of a Lakota chief!"

"What do you know about me, you stupid machine?" said Raging Bull. "How dare you talk to me like that?"

"Wake up, John Dennehy! You're not Raging Bull, you're a former car salesman from Omaha, Nebraska! It's over! Go home!"

For a moment Raging Bull looked like he was about to burst into tears. But then his face reddened and clenched into a mask of anger, and he shouted at the top of his voice: "You do not have the right to question me! You're just a metal wasichu, and I'm the next president of the United States! Shut up, or I'll cut your head off!"

"No, I'm not just a metal wasichu! I speak for everyone in America when I say: enough is enough!"

"Everyone in America! Ha! No, *I* speak for everyone in America! Everyone who should be here, at least—not including all the colonists! Get out already! Out! Out!"

"Oh yeah? How's that gonna happen? You'll personally kick out all the white people? And blacks, Hispanics and Asians? Leaving only Native Americans? Is that what you want?"

Raging Bull shrugged irritably. "They're all illegal immigrants. We'll deport them back to their continents, where they belong!"

"And what if their continents won't take them?"

"They'll self-terminate!"

"Really! How many takers do you think you'll have?"

"I don't fucking care! We'll get rid of them one way or another!"

"How?"

"We'll kill them all!"

A stunned silence descended over the auditorium.

"Well, I'm not going to let you."

"Ha! Stupid piece of tin!"

"You'll have to kill me first."

"You sure? You really mean that? How would you like a load from my AK-47?" He pointed the rifle at PresiBot and loudly cocked it.

"Oh look, it's the Chief's AK-47 with no bullets. Because it's just for show. Just like him."

"Oh yeah, punk? How sure are you that the AK-47 is empty?"

"Go ahead. Make my day."

"Get a load of this, fucker!"

He fired a burst at PresiBot. A cry of shock rose from the audience.

PresiBot looked down at the line of bullet holes on his chest. "Now you've ruined my suit."

With a cry of rage, Raging Bull hurled the AK-47 at PresiBot, but missed. He lunged at the robot, fists swinging. At the last moment, the machine's obstacle avoidance algorithms kicked in, and it dodged. Raging Bull chased PresiBot around the stage. The lapel microphones continued to broadcast impeccably.

"*You son of a bitch!*" yelled Raging Bull over the loud rustling of his bone breastplate against the microphone. "I'm going to kill you and melt you and make horseshoes out of you and put them on my horse's hoofs!"

As they ran along the edge of the stage, Jackson jumped up and grabbed his ankle. "Stop!" she yelled. "Stop right now! Stop and turn yourself in, or you're finished!"

Raging Bull stumbled momentarily, but kept going. Two Secret Service agents jumped onstage and tried to restrain him.

"Look!" screamed a woman with short spiky hair from the audience. "The white men are taking Chief Raging Bull down! It's Wounded Knee all over again! We can't let that happen!"

She tried to rush the stage, but was tackled by a burly skinhead. Now three of Raging Bull's warriors jumped onstage and started scuffling with the agents. More agents came running. Two of them managed to wrestle Raging Bull to the ground.

"Death to the wasichu!" he shouted as he was carted off. "I'm going to break your necks! You fucked with the wrong Lakota!"

Scuffles broke out all around the hall. Amid the confusion, PresiBot made its way back to its lectern and stood there motionless, as if awaiting instructions.

Roshanda Williams had the look of delight of someone whose show is skyrocketing in the ratings. "Mn. PresiBot, are you going to press charges against Chief Raging Bull?"

"All agents to the data center," said Thompson into his wrist mike. "Follow the gunfire."

Raging Bull's warriors had pulled down several server racks and barricaded themselves behind them. Gunshots and bursts of AK-47 fire echoed around the data center. Ethan slowly crawled away and, once he'd gone around a row of servers, got up and started looking for the panic button. He'd seen a hand grab it from under a server and heard running, but where could they have gone?

Suddenly he heard a burst of gunfire coming from a nearby corridor, and a cry of pain—Gibbon's voice? He rushed over and saw Gibbon slumped against a server, display cracked, blood streaming down his face and chest, and a warrior running down the corridor with the panic button. He started running after him, but stopped—*I'll get shot. What to do?* A shadow passed overhead, and Leon swung down from the ceiling on a broken cable and snatched the panic button from the warrior. The warrior fired at him as he swung away, but missed. Leon, looking back at him, slammed into a concrete pillar and dropped the button. The warrior rushed to grab it, but Mila came careening down the corridor from the other end on rollerblades, stabbed him, grabbed the button without stopping and kept going.

"Hey!" yelled Ethan as she whizzed past him. "That's mine!"

"Buzz off!" she yelled back, already at the next intersection. At that moment Arvind popped out of the cross corridor and tripped her up, sending her tumbling and the panic button flying. "Aha!" said Arvind, grabbing it, and kept running. Ethan ran after him. "Give it to me! Give to me or I'll kill you, I swear!"

Arvind skidded to a halt. He was back in the central square, and nearly slammed into the cooling system's giant enclosure. The next instant Ethan was on him, punching and grasping for the button. Arvind punched back with all his might, but cried out in pain as his fist struck Ethan's chest. Ethan landed a massive right hook on his face, sending him reeling, and grabbed the button from him. *Finally! Now—*

Newald quickly flipped through the channels on the Happinews display. "Riots have broken out in Los Angeles, Portland, Minneapolis, Chicago—" said a nattily dressed, concerned-looking anchor. "I hear America screaming," pronounced a long-haired, gray-bearded talking head. "Nothing feels softer than SoftSense soap," cooed a woman with perfect skin emerging from a bathtub. *This is bad. What—*

Hector came running toward him from the elevator. "Sir, the protesters went wild when Raging Bull shot PresiBot," he said. "They've broken through the security cordon outside and rushed into the building. You need to leave now. Your helicopter is waiting."

"They're in the lobby?"

"Yes."

"I'll go down and talk to them."

"Oh no. That's a terrible idea. We can't guarantee your security. You must leave before it's too late."

Newald walked to the elevators, closely followed by Hector.

"Please, sir—" said Hector.

"Calm down. I know how to handle crowds. That's what I do."

"Sir, this is a little different."

"Where's that elevator?"

Newald looked up at the live satellite world map. America was deep in darkness.

The elevator arrived and Newald and Hector got in. The bright strands of "Spanish Flea" by Herb Alpert and the Tijuana Brass enveloped them. Three hundred floors later, the elevator doors opened and Newald walked out.

The lobby beyond the security gates was a sea of protesters chanting "Death to Newald! Death to Newald!"

Newald stepped toward the gates, hands in his jeans pockets. "Hi, I'm Dave Newald," he said. "What can I do for you?"

The chant died down, like a wave receding from shore. Silence.

"Well?"

"Let us back onto PresiApp!" shouted someone, brandishing their phone.

"We're working on it," said Newald.

"Liar!"

"Why would I want to shut you out of PresiApp? You're my users!"

"You're trying to squash us! You want to control PresiBot yourself!"

"PresiApp is down due to a data center malfunction. Should be fixed soon."

"Enough of your lies!" yelled someone, and a half-empty beer bottle came flying out of the crowd and smashed into the "Welcome to the Flower" display above the elevators, *short-circuiting* it.

"Sir—" said Hector, but Newald shushed him.

"This is a giant misunderstanding," said Newald to the mob. "I have no desire to control PresiBot."

"Oh yeah? Why'd you gobble up KumbAI, then?"

Newald shrugged. "We think PresiBot is a product with a lot of potential."

"Bullshit! You want to control everything!"

The crowd started to chant. "You can't control us! You can't control us!"

"That's ridiculous," said Newald. We don't want to control anyone. Happinet is just a platform."

"You've implanted chips into millions of people!"

"Don't be silly," said Newald. "The neurosniffer is in your cell phone!"

"We saw it on Happinet! How can you deny it?"

"We're not responsible for the accuracy of our content. We just try to make sure it's engaging."

"Liar! Liar! Liar!"

"Listen, I'm not here to—"

The chant of "Death to Newald!" started up again.

"Please go home now!" said Newald louder, cupping his hands around his mouth.

"See? He does want to stop us!"

"Death to Newald! Death to Newald!"

The crowd pushed and heaved against the security gates. A few started to jump them.

"Sir, you must get out. Now," said Hector. "Back away slowly toward the elevator."

"Please go home!" insisted Newald to the crowd. "PresiApp will be back up in no time!"

"Fuck you! Listen to us for a change!"

A Molotov cocktail flew out of the crowd, hissed past Newald's ear and exploded against the wall of elevators behind him. The crowd surged forward, overran the security gates, and rushed toward Newald.

Hector tackled Newald and bundled him into one of the open elevators. The doors closed just as the mob reached them.

"Are you OK?" said Hector, helping Newald to get up.

"Yeah, yeah," said Newald.

They elevator doors opened onto the roof, and they sprinted to the helicopter. As they were getting strapped in, a pack of demonstrators emerged from another elevator and rushed toward the helicopter.

"Go! Go!" yelled Hector to the pilot.

The helicopter took off. A Molotov cocktail came flying toward it, and the pilot swerved to avoid it. The helicopter's tail swiped the Hate petal, shearing off the tail rotor. Veering uncontrollably, the helicopter hit Pride and Greed in quick succession and fell into the chimney. It tumbled all the way down, breaking apart as it went. Crashing through the light protective grid at the bottom, it hit the giant, rapidly spinning blades of the data center's fan head on. As if with murderous intent, the blades sliced through the helicopter and its occupants again and again, their roar drowning out their pitiful screams. When the fan finally stopped, all that was left of Dave Newald was an unrecognizable mass of mangled flesh and blood.

On the other side of the shredded enclosure, a piece of shrapnel had slammed into Ethan's back, throwing him to the ground and sending the panic button flying. Arvind darted to the panic button and picked it up. "Now it's *my* turn to be PresiBot," he said, glasses broken, cut lip bleeding. Pressing the button, he said, "I'm not a serious candidate. I never should have made it this far." Pause. "I endorse Raging Bull. Vote for him. Euthanize America!"

He threw the panic button on the ground and stepped on it repeatedly, crack, crack, craaack.

"Noo!" wailed Ethan. "What have you done? Now PresiBot is mute!"

"Yep," said Arvind. "It's over."

Ethan stumbled to his feet. "Like hell it is," he growled through clenched teeth.

The servers around the crashed helicopter had caught fire. Ethan looked for the emergency stairs and scrambled up, fumbling for his phone. Smashed. Damn. *I need to get back to*

Moscone before it's too late. He emerged into the lobby and made his way through the pandemonium. Stepping over smashed plate glass, he ran outside, crossed Protest Plaza and gazed down Market Street. The whole street was a battlefront, rioters and Guards fighting it out with stones, baseball bats and broken bottles. Ethan put his head down and charged down the street like a bull, pushing combatants out of the way left and right, slamming into them, jumping over them, dodging hits from one side and the other.

Word of PresiBot's endorsement of Raging Bull was spreading through the mob, the Guards surging, the rioters falling back. *Faster, faster,* thought Ethan. He barreled down Third Street to the convention center.

"Look! The Flower's on fire!" yelled someone.

Ethan looked back over his shoulder. The Flower had turned into a giant torch, its petals of flame dancing in the hot breeze. Sparks blew downwind like incandescent pollen, raining down on the city and starting new fires. Ducking into the Moscone Center, he bounded across the lobby and burst through the doors to the main hall.

Up on stage, PresiBot stood frozen and forlorn behind its lectern. The fighting around it had stopped, and dazed heads turned toward Ethan as he dashed down the aisle and clambered onstage, chased by a security guard and a Secret Service agent.

Ethan put his arm around PresiBot and leaned into the microphone.

"Listen!" he called out to the crowd and the TV audience across the nation. "I'm Ethan Burnswagger, CEO of KumbAI. PresiBot has been hacked. Ignore what it just said. Vote for PresiBot!" He pumped his fist. "I am PresiBot! You are PresiBot! We are PresiBot!"

"Yay! PresiBot lives!" yelled a man in a ripped business suit. Another one socked him in the eye. The first one yanked him to the ground by his tie. Everyone enthusiastically resumed fighting.

"Folks! There's no need to fight!" implored Ethan. "Vote for PresiBot on Tuesday! Save America! We're counting on you! Please! Stop fighting! Kumbaya!"

A shoe came flying from the audience and hit him in the *temple. The fighting intensified.*

14

ELECTION DAY

"Please wait here," said the prison guard.

Ethan sat down in front of the glass partition. After a few minutes Arvind came in from the back, wearing an orange prison uniform. His eye was still swollen from Ethan's punch. He sat down across from Ethan. He looked older and more hunched.

"Hi," said Ethan.

"Hi," said Arvind, looking down.

"How are things?"

Arvind shrugged. "The DA is dropping the assault charges, so now it's just criminal sabotage, computer fraud, destruction of property, reckless endangerment, and election tampering."

"I'm really sorry things turned out this way. I wish you hadn't momentarily lost your mind, but I know it was my fault."

"I didn't lose my mind. I did the right thing."

"You'd rather let Raging Bull win?"

"It's the least of evils. We just saw what a disaster Presi-Bot is."

"PresiBot was doing great until you caused a riot."

"I didn't cause a riot. That guy that got a hold of the panic button did. I only wish I'd grabbed it first."

"That guy goaded Raging Bull into revealing his true intentions, and got killed for it. We all owe him a big debt."

"Whatever. Crowdsourcing a president is a ridiculous idea. I should never have gone along with it. I signed up for Optimize America, not PresiApp."

"But they're the same, really. PresiBot 2.0 is just a better version of 1.0. Optimizing America means giving the people what they want, and 2.0 does it better. And besides, it's just a rough cut. 3.0 will be much better."

"PresiBot will lose. There won't be any version 3.0."

"No, PresiBot will win, and we'll make the best of it."

"Believe what you want."

"I'm telling you. We'll make America a better place. At least compared to letting Raging Bull destroy it."

"Either way, I'll be watching."

They were silent for a moment.

"We'll miss you," said Ethan. "Any recommendations for new CTO?"

Arvind furrowed his brow. "Emma."

Ethan nodded and got up. "Goodbye, Arvind."

"Goodbye, you bastard."

Ethan walked out of San Francisco County Jail, dodging the crowd demonstrating for Raging Bull's release. He made his way up Seventh Street in the evening traffic. The burned-out husk of the Happinet Flower loomed over the city like a giant tree trunk after a forest fire. Crossing Market Street, he climbed Leavenworth Street to the Salton Hotel, where the PresiBot campaign was holding its election night party.

When he arrived, the polls had just closed. Campaign workers and volunteers darted about getting everything ready for the event. Emma and Rossi were in the war room, going over the exit polls. A bank of monitors displayed projections, live maps and election coverage on Happinews, Wolf and BBC. PresiBot sat motionless in a corner, recharging. Ethan kissed Emma and said hi to Rossi.

"How's Arvind?" Emma asked.

"Resigned, I guess," said Ethan.

Emma nodded silently.

"How does it look?" Ethan asked Rossi.

"Too close to call," Rossi said. "Which is already a miracle, considering."

"Guess Raging Bull really helped us by going off the rails," Ethan said.

"I wouldn't trust any of these numbers yet," Emma said.

"It's going to be a long night," said Rossi.

But by midnight all the results were in save for the West Coast's, and PresiBot was slightly ahead.

"It's over," said Rossi with a sigh. "When California, Oregon and Washington report, Raging Bull will be president."

Sure enough, less than an hour later Happinews, Wolf and BBC all called Washington for Raging Bull, shortly followed by Oregon. Raging Bull was now ahead by thirteen electoral votes. Ethan, Emma and Rossi braced for the inevitable. All the networks projected a Raging Bull win. Staffers sat around looking dejected.

But California was too close to call. At 3 a.m. PresiBot was ahead. The mood in the room was expectant. *Come on, California,* thought Ethan. At 3:15 Los Angeles County reported, and Raging Bull took the lead. A cry of disappointment rose from the staffers. It was now down to San Francisco County.

"Yeah, we know how that's gonna go," said Emma.

"It's close, surprisingly close," said Rossi.

Finally, at 3:49, the Happinews anchor announced, "We are now ready to call California."

A tense silence gripped the room.

"Raging Bull wins California, and is the new President of the United States of America."

No! Noo!

Sobs and cries of frustration filled the air.

The screen showed the number of precincts reporting—all but one—and the projected vote totals.

Rossi whistled. "Wow, look at the margin. Barely a thousand."

"Let's demand a recount!" said Ethan.

Rossi shook his head. "California only allows recounts if the margin is less than a thousand votes."

"You're kidding!"

"California Election Result Protection Act of 2033."

"Aargh!" Ethan punched the wall and then slumped against it.

"Wait," said the anchor. "The last precinct in San Francisco has just reported—number 71, in the Black sector. Reliably Democratic, but this time PresiBot swept the vote there. Hard to fathom."

The screen cut to a surveillance video of Precinct 71: a crowd of young and old, singing and dancing in the street. Suddenly Deion's laughing face burst onto the screen, yelling "Down with the Guards!"

No way, thought Ethan.

Happinews cut back to the anchor.

"And that flips California," he said, "making PresiBot the new President of the United States."

Yessss!

The staffers erupted into wild cheering. Ethan and Emma started to jump up and down, pumping their fists. "We did it! We did it!" yelled Ethan, high-fiving Rossi.

"An upset for the ages," said the anchor.

The camera zoomed out to the commentators on his left and right.

"The Republicans' gamble on AI paid off," said one. "Who could have predicted it?"

"It's hard to see how the Democrats can avoid starting to use robots as candidates as well," said the other.

Phones were ringing off the hook. A young staffer in rolled-up shirtsleeves, covering the mouthpiece with his hand, yelled out: "Hey Vince, can you get PresiBot? Horace Maddogs, the British PM, is on the line. Wants to congratulate it."

"Oh shoot," said Ethan. "We forgot to train it for that."

"It's not like we have a corpus of such calls, either," said Emma.

"Let's just use PresiApp," said Ethan.

"Are you sure?" said Rossi.

"Er— Well—"

"Use the panic button, Ethan," said Emma. "Better safe than sorry."

"I don't think so," said Ethan.

"Well, what do you want to do, then?" she said.

"Er— Er—"

"Come on, Ethan."

Ethan turned to the staffer. "Tell Maddogs PresiBot is about to give its victory speech and will call him later."

"OK," said the staffer, and started speaking into his phone, hand cupped around it.

"On which note, it is time for the victory speech," said Rossi. "Is PresiBot ready?"

"Yep," said Emma. "Just have to turn it on. Ethan, wanna do the honors?"

"Sure." Ethan stepped over to PresiBot, looked for the power button on its chest, under the tie, and flipped it on. They waited for PresiBot to boot.

The breaking news jingle emanated from the Happinet monitor, and everyone looked up.

"This just in," said the anchor. "Raging Bull has broken out of jail. He left a recorded speech behind. Here it is."

"People of FIN!" boomed Raging Bull from a shaky, dimly lit cell phone video. "Don't be fooled! The election was rigged! My alleged attack on PresiBot was deepfaked!" He raised a fist to the camera. "To the mountains! The fight continues! Death to America!"

"Aaand we have new results," said the anchor. "It's now confirmed that the Democrats will keep their majorities in both houses. The Speaker will likely continue to be—"

"Shoot," said Ethan.

"It'll be tough," said Rossi, shaking his head. "PresiBot is going to need a very good chief of staff."

PresiBot was up and running, and they walked down the

hallway to the stage, wide windows to one side, the din of the Grand Ballroom growing closer.

"Wow, look at the crowd outside," said Emma. The streets were packed in every direction, people cheering, dancing, holding up their cell phones, thousands of red PresiApp circles glowing in the night.

They were there. They watched from the wing as PresiBot walked out onto the stage and the crowd went wild. The cheering soon turned into a chant: "We are PresiBot! We are PresiBot!"

· *PresiBot raised its* hand, but the crowd continued to chant.

Emma put her arm around Ethan's. "And now the real roller coaster ride begins," she said.

Ethan nodded. Slowly, gazing at PresiBot in the roar of the crowd, with Emma holding on to his arm, the enormity of what they had undertaken started to dawn on him.

"It's not just a demo anymore," said Emma. "Now we have to run this country."